Messenger

OF

THE

GODS

Printed in Australia

Cover and internal design by Shawline Publishing Group Pty Ltd

First printing: July 2024

Shawline Publishing Group Pty Ltd

www.shawlinepublishing.com.au

Paperback ISBN 978-1-9231-7127-5

eBook ISBN 978-1-9231-7139-8

Hardback ISBN 978-1-9231-7151-0

Distributed by Shawline Distribution and Lightning Source Global

Shawline Publishing Group acknowledges the traditional owners of the land and pays respects to Elders, past, present and future.

A catalogue record for this work is available from the National Library of Australia

TIMOTHY GERRARD

Messenger
of
the
Gods

To Peg

1

I thought my scar was itching again. I say 'scar' in the singular as the long red and purple line that ran from my neck, just below the left ear, diagonally down and across my chest and abdomen, and then the length of my right leg to below the ankle was an ugly mess of tortured flesh. The irony was that I had put it there myself by tumbling from the howdah of a war elephant. My fall had taken me onto and across the great battle sword attached to the elephant's tusk and thus had opened me up – literally – from head to toe. Had a team of physicians and surgeons been on hand, the scar might have been a relatively neat suture line.

It was definitely not a neat suture line. There had been no needles, no threads of silk, no artery clamps; only red-hot embers to cauterise the many pulsing blood vessels down the length of my body. I was lucky to be unconscious at the time and do not recall any of this. I was told much later that I bucked and jerked with each placement of the burning embers, despite being senseless. Consequently, my scar has all the ridges, craters, wrinkles, folds, bulges and puckerings that can be seen on those who have been severely burned. It was still an angry-looking slash, as it was still mending, awaiting the day when my body's healing processes would see it take on the normal colour of skin, albeit somewhat paler and less elastic in nature.

The healing process may seem a good thing; the damaged body is repaired, reshaped and taken back, as much as possible, to its original strong and healthy state. Except it isn't always that pleasant. There are burning sensations that accompany inflammation, tearing sensations that can come from a careless movement – a cough, a laugh or a sneeze – as well as unscratchable and irritating tinglings beneath the surface of the scar and an almost ever-present itch at some spot along its entire length.

I was lying on my back and looking down the length of the bedsheet across my waist to where the itch on my right ankle was located. I was just about to cross my left leg over my right and scratch the spot with my toenails when I saw a small bulge in the sheet move. The itchy sensation moved with it. With a shock, I realised something – some animal or insect – was in the bed I shared with my beloved, Ruth, and was furtively making its way up my leg. In Hind, I knew this could be very bad, even fatal. I gingerly raised the sheet an inch or two to peep under the cover, and my worst fear was realised. There, above my ankle, I could just make out the shape of a four-inch scorpion. A small shiver of horror ran down my spine.

There was just enough light in the room for me to note its dull grey body, its six reddy-orange legs, its two large pincers and its slightly raised and painfully deadly stinging tail. I gently lowered the sheet, keeping its weight upon my toes, rather than letting it settle on the ugly little beast, so as not to startle it and possibly cause it to unleash its sting into me.

My first concern was for Ruth, who was lying naked and asleep beside me. We had made very slow and gentle love to each other earlier in the night, with her taking the superior position, as she had on all previous occasions. My healing wound did not allow me to take a more dominant or vigorous role in our lovemaking. I knew my genitals would still be moist from the experience.

I was concerned that any sudden movement would cause the

scorpion to whip its stinging tail into my leg. I slowly turned my head to Ruth's side of the bed and whispered, 'Ruth. Ruth,' as softly as I could. No response.

The scorpion moved a little further up my calf. Beads of sweat started to form on my forehead.

'Ruth. Ruth,' I whispered again.

The scorpion crept slowly upward, finally stopping just above my knee. I could feel its tiny, pointed feet moving over my skin, gently pricking me as it went. I began to break out in a real sweat, all over my body.

'Mmmh,' mumbled Ruth, still half asleep.

'Don't move. Don't say or do anything suddenly,' I said, trying to make my whisper sound as real and as urgent as the situation. 'Just lie still, very still. There is a scorpion in our bed.'

Ruth did not consciously move or make a sound, but her minute, startled reflex sent a small ripple along the sheet. I felt the scorpion scuttle quickly up the inside of my thigh, only to stop in what it possibly thought was some kind of protective and bushy camouflage.

Fear and horror of its current location kept me absolutely frozen.

The sheet lay only partially across my pubic area, and I was able to observe much of the scorpion's activity. Slowly, its stinging tail came down into a less threatening position and it seemed to begin investigating its surroundings. After a moment, the little beast stopped moving around and settled with its head against the base of my penis, its pincer claws closed but placed around the flaccid flesh in an embrace. I began to feel a slight rasping sensation against the surface of the skin there.

Is it feeding on, or cleaning, the residue of the love Ruth and I made earlier? I wondered. From the little movements around the scorpion's mouth, I suspected the former. It was not a pleasant idea.

I became aware that ever so gently, ever so slowly, Ruth was sidling over to the edge of the bed. The scorpion continued its oral activity, but I could feel its sharp little feet and pincers periodically moving their way around the warm and still slightly moistened environment it was hiding in.

Gradually, Ruth removed the sheet from our bodies and let it lie beside me without provoking the creature. With frequent pauses, she moved her legs over the side of the bed and her feet onto the floor. It was when she lifted her buttocks and attempted to stand that the mattress rippled with the movement. Immediately, the scorpion's tail went up into striking position, and I braced myself for the sting of death. It did not come. Instead, the scorpion changed position so that it now lay across my very shrunken penis. All I could do was look down the length of my torso at this vile creature. It seemed to be staring back up at me angrily as it tried to disentangle its legs from my pubic hairs.

The creature had several eyes, two large ones in front and five smaller ones sitting further back across its forehead. From either side of the head reached two pincers, miniature versions of a lobster's claws that, along with its forelegs, were still entangled in my pubic hairs. This seemed to agitate the creature, as it struggled to release itself. Its tail came up yet again.

I was in a state of silent horror when I felt the movement in my bowels that accompanies intense terror. I had experienced these sensations before going into battle at Gadaraghatta a few weeks before. I looked across to where Ruth was quietly removing one of her slender throwing knives from its belted sheath. She usually wore the belt across her chest, but it was now lying on her bedside table.

Uncontrollably, my bowels made a sudden deep gurgling sound. The scorpion's tail arched. Its stinger rose further and was about to strike when a flashing blur sped over my penis. There was a sharp sting and a woody thump. The scorpion had disappeared, pinned by Ruth's throwing knife to the side of my bedside table, its legs and pincers waving angrily around in the air.

I looked down again at my manhood to see a tiny drop of blood welling from the small nick made by Ruth's throwing knife. A great, rumbling fart trumpeted from my bowels.

I had just got off very, very lightly.

2

'It is definitely a red scorpion, and, I might say, a rather large one,' said Kali, examining the insect, which was still on the point of Ruth's knife, although it was no longer moving. 'It is notoriously aggressive, and its poison will kill a man within twenty-four hours. This is always accompanied by many painful horrors, with the victim finally drowning in their own body fluids. Truly horrible.'

He paused briefly and scratched his chin.

'I would not like to die that way. Nor would I wish it on any other.'

My travelling companions, Hadar, Caspar, Raymond, and Kali, had been quickly summoned from their nearby rooms by Ruth and were now gathered around my bed just a short while after the unexpected visitation.

'My concern is, how did that wretched scorpion come to be in the hospital?' said Hadar. 'And, what's more, up here on the third level? I doubt it climbed the stairs, and it's certainly a large enough creature to have been noticed. There's something not quite right about all of this.'

The creases and lines on his forehead furrowed and deepened.

'I agree. Given the hospital's daily cleaning, washing of floors and high standards of hygiene, it does seem very suspicious,' remarked Ruth.

'More so,' interjected Kali, 'in that the red scorpion is not usually found in this part of Hind. It's more common in the eastern regions around Bengal and the coast.'

We all became silent as the unpleasant ramifications of the scorpion's appearance in the bed Ruth and I shared became apparent.

'My instincts tell me we must definitely be on our guard,' said Caspar gravely. 'I do not think it is safe for Ippolito and Ruth to be left alone. Raymond and I shall mount a permanent rotational armed guard at your door. Night and day. Perhaps, Kali, you might help out as well?'

Kali nodded.

'A good idea,' pronounced Hadar, 'but let us ask, who has been in the room already? That may give us some clues as to our malefactor's identity. Ippolito, Ruth. Who else has been here in the last two or three days?'

Ruth and I looked at each other, casting our memory back over the last few days.

'Well, everyday cleaners, orderlies, catering staff and the like come in and out as a matter of hospital routine,' I began. 'Indra and Deva are the two cleaners, but they're chubby middle-aged women with families. I somehow don't think they would be likely assassins, let alone scorpion handlers.'

Ruth nodded. 'I doubt that any of the catering staff would've had the time or the opportunity to secrete a scorpion in here. They're too busy bustling around, getting all the meals out on time. As for orderlies and assistants, Kali and I have attended to all of Ippolito's personal and hygiene needs.'

'Mmmh. That rules the regular hospital staff out,' said Hadar, stroking his beard. 'Who has visited you, aside from those of us here?'

'It was only yesterday that the queen, accompanied by Narmala and four horse guards, was in this room. It was her second visit that I know of since I regained my senses. She sat at my bedside,

Narmala and Ruth just behind her, and we chatted for an hour or so. The four guards were stationed around the room, by the door and the windows.'

Ruth chortled. 'And the rest, Ippolito?'

'The queen said she wanted to run her hand down the length of my scar and feel its ridges and bumps,' I said with some embarrassment.

'And did she?' interjected Raymond with a grin.

'Most of it. Not all. I can assure you my loincloth stayed in place,' I replied, smiling.

'Any other visitors?' pressed Hadar.

'Various physicians and healers have examined Ruth's handiwork on my body, but every one of them was accompanied by you,' I said.

'It seems unlikely to have been any of your visitors or hospital staff,' concluded Hadar, 'but we cannot rule them out entirely.'

'We did upset and terrify quite a number of guests at the queen's dinner when we first arrived here,' offered Raymond. 'Do you suppose any of them might harbour thoughts of revenge?'

'They would be taking a mighty big risk, should Queen Naiki Devi learn of such treachery,' responded Hadar. 'Remember the ranter's fate, and the other executions by elephant's foot and trunk before the battle at Gadaraghatta. I'm sure the queen in her wrath would devise some horrendous demise for any who tried to harm her precious blue and red demons.'

'There is one agent we have not considered,' said Caspar, 'and that is Mohammed of Ghor. Most certainly he has spies and agents operating here in Anhilwara Patan and possibly in the queen's palace as well. After his humiliating defeat at the hands of the queen and our two young demons here, he may be seeking his revenge. He may not be able to reach the queen with his assassins in the palace, but he can reach into the hospital.'

Caspar moved over to the window and looked down. 'There are multiple handholds amidst the carvings and adornments that decorate the walls. An assassin could easily scale them at night and enter through the window.'

He shook his head grimly.

'After the ignominy of his defeat, particularly with the flaming pigs and the flying piglets that Raymond and I launched, Ghor will be a laughing-stock amongst his Moslem co-rulers. He will want revenge as quickly as possible so as to save face within his realm and hang on to his throne. I can assure you some Moslem prince or other royal notable will have their eye on it. Ghor may even hire the services of that old rogue Alaeddin Mohammed Sabah and his assassins to do the job for him.'

This was unsettling news to Ruth and me, to think that we were being targeted for death by any means possible. And there was I, only just beginning to recover some of my strength and mobility, with a long road of healing in front of me.

'Clearly,' said Hadar, 'we must maintain a strong vigilance, and' – he added with emphasis – 'get this young man up on his feet and moving again as quickly as possible.'

Ruth looked at me with a knowing and secret grin. 'Well, he is getting stronger and faster at some things.'

Raymond laughed. 'Too much information!'

3

After our meeting had finished and everyone had dispersed – Hadar and Kali to the hospital clinic, and Caspar to the armoury – Raymond remained behind, not only to act as a guard but also to assist Ruth in my twice-daily massage and rehabilitation regime.

One of the problems with scarring from burns is that the scar tissue contracts into ropey lengths, which lack the elasticity of normal skin, and thus impede the body's normal range of movement. For instance, the scar tissue down the left side of my neck restricted my turning my head to the right side, as it would be pulled so taut no further movement was possible. The scarring that continued diagonally down my chest and abdomen impeded my ability to take a full breath, such as one might take before diving into water. Twisting and turning my upper body from the hips was also a problem for me. The same stubborn scar tissue down my right leg affected my ability to walk, run, squat, sit and rise. While my right side and its sword arm were unaffected, it was seriously let down by the limitations of the rest of my body. I doubted I would ever regain the swordsmanship I had so painfully learned from Edward and Caspar.

Hadar had said it was important to treat the scar both medicinally and physically. He had acquired an Ayurvedic preparation he claimed was highly recommended by some of his Hind colleagues at the hospital. He explained that the preparation had two properties: the first to impart greater elasticity to the scar tissue and the second to provide a degree of analgesia to the tissues prior to the painful stretches and kneading of the physical treatment that I had to endure.

My twice-daily treatment began with Ruth placing hot, moist towels along the length of the scar. This was to open the pores of my skin, allowing greater penetration of the elasticising and analgesic ingredients of the Ayurvedic preparation. Ruth would use her thumbs to knead the ointment into me by pressing down hard and moving them in a rolling motion along the surface of the scar. This was initially quite painful, as I could feel the flesh pulling and tearing under the pressure of her thumbs. After a few minutes, the pain would somewhat abate as the preparation began to leach into the scar and take effect. It was not much in the way of relief, but I hate to think of the pain the physical treatment would have caused me without it. The physical treatment was torture.

Raymond was required to perform the 'torture', as Ruth, being a young woman, was simply not physically strong enough to put my body through what Hadar and his Ayurvedic medical colleagues recommended for me. I also suspect that Ruth did not want to have to hurt me in any way. In fact, Ruth would leave the room, not so much because she could not bear to see the pain I was put through but rather to avoid hearing the curses, profanities and threats that Raymond and I bandied around during the painful stretching process.

'You really are a stiff-necked goose, Ippolito. Relax,' quipped Raymond as he turned my head further to the right than I could myself, sending white-hot bolts of pain shooting down the left side of my neck.

'It isn't *your* head that's being pulled off! You're worse than Bhari

Pair, the executioner's elephant,' I retorted, remembering the heads that had been separated from their bodies by that particular elephant's trunk.

Raymond twisted my neck a little further.

'Arrgh!' I bellowed. 'That really hurt, you bloody dog's turd.'

'Yes. I hope it did, you pissy little girl. But your neck has just turned further around than yesterday. By the time I'm done with this, you'll be able to look up your arse.'

This made us both laugh, and somehow, my torture did not seem so bad – but only for a minute or two. Raymond moved along the bedside and grasped my right ankle.

'You know the drill. Grab the bedhead rail and hang on,' he said.

'You make it sound like a sordid little love tryst. You really are a deviant and sadistic bastard,' came my reply.

Slowly, Raymond pulled on my ankle, stretching my leg and its scar out as he held it there for what seemed like a hell-born eternity, before releasing the ankle and letting the muscles and scar tissue relax. Then he repeated the process several times over, with various twists and turns of my ankle and leg that would pull and stretch the scar in a dozen different painful directions.

'I hope you treat your women better than this,' I said between grunts of sweating pain.

'Not exactly. But they all come back for more.'

Raymond did not have to guide the stretching of the scar along my torso. I could do this myself, with him giving encouragement to twist and turn further and hold the painful position for longer and longer. Only occasionally would Raymond assist by holding me in the position I had reached, before releasing me from the aching tremor that shook itself down the entire length of my body.

The final part of this torture was the re-application of the hot towels and Ayurvedic ointment. Raymond vigorously and painfully massaged it into the scar, where its elasticising properties could leach down to the torn and traumatised tissues below. As before, the discomfort was somewhat relieved by the analgesic ingredients of the ointment.

I lay there in silence, glad that this part of the day was over and also dreading that later that afternoon, I would have to go through it all again. Still, I could tell I was making progress with my recovery.

A cheeky thought came into my head. Perhaps tonight, I might be able to surprise Ruth with something new in our physical relationship.

4

Later that night, Ruth and I were lying quietly, basking in the left-over warm glow of our lovemaking, when we heard urgent voices outside the bedroom door. We quickly pulled the sheet up to cover our nakedness as Narmala silently and quickly led Hadar, Caspar, Raymond and Kali into the room. I noticed each of them, with the exception of Narmala, had what looked like hastily packed travel bags with them. Raymond was also carrying Hadar's medical supply kit.

'I will explain later,' said Narmala urgently. 'We must get you dressed and away from here as quickly as possible. Caspar, watch the door. Raymond, the windows. Hadar. Kali. Look the other way.'

They all quickly did as Narmala requested, and she whipped the sheet off the bed, revealing Ruth and me in all our naked glory.

'Get dressed, Ruth, and then gather a few belongings for a fast exit.'

Narmala went to the closet shelf and pulled an old kaftan of mine from it. 'Arms above your head,' she ordered snappily, and she tugged the kaftan down the length of my body. Then she amazed me with her strength by sliding one hand under my buttocks and lifting me from the bed, while with the other, she pulled the kaftan underneath me, without interfering with what hung below.

In another swift motion, she placed one hand under my legs, the other behind my back, and swung me around so that I was sitting on the side of the bed before I knew it. What was more amazing was that she managed all of this while only causing me a minimal amount of pain.

'Ipp,' she said authoritatively, 'you can't keep up with us, so we're going to have to drag or carry you out of here.'

I was suddenly reminded of our passage dragging the wounded Godfrey on a palliasse from the assassins' fortress, the Eagle's Nest. So much had happened since then; it seemed a lifetime ago.

'Okay. But why? What's happening?' I queried.

'It's the queen. She wants you both dead.'

Ruth and I stared at each other in shock and bewilderment as Narmala gathered the sheets from the bed and laid them on the floor. Then Narmala quickly and gently manhandled me to land upon the sheets, her hands behind my back to cushion the tumble. I was surprised that she could accomplish such speed while still ensuring my comfort and safety.

'Caspar. Raymond. Grab the sheet and start dragging Ippolito,' she said, pointing to the end where my head lay. 'Quickly now. All of you, follow me, and don't make a sound.'

With that, Narmala was out the door and leading the way along the hospital corridor. I looked up at the ceiling going by above me and then around at my colleagues. Ruth was striding protectively by my side, a worried look upon her face, and glancing around every so often. Behind me, Hadar and Kali were encouraging each other to keep up. I couldn't see Narmala, Caspar or Raymond in front of the sheet. No one made a sound as we hurried down the corridor.

From the ceiling, I could tell we had come to an open area of the hospital floor. It was the top of the stairway. There didn't seem to be any staff around, as all was silent.

'Raymond. Caspar. Be ready on my command to take the weight

of the sheet up onto your shoulders,' whispered Narmala. 'Ruth. Get beside me and grab the other corner of the sheet.'

Ruth did so, and I realised I was about to be stretchered down three flights of stairs. I hoped everyone held tight.

'Ready, and up!' whispered Narmala.

I felt myself raised from the floor, with my head higher than my feet by a foot or two.

'All of you,' directed Narmala, 'listen for my tempo as we go down the stairs. And do it softly and silently.' She put particular emphasis on the last word.

Suddenly, my feet rose in front of me, and I felt myself being carried down the stairs step by step to Narmala's whispered tempo of, 'One, two, one, two.' It was a very smooth ride, considering the difficulties.

My position changed at the landings between and on each floor as we levelled out, turned and changed direction. It was not long before we arrived at the ground floor and I was again being dragged along by Caspar and Raymond. Narmala led the way to the rear of the hospital and guided us out through a rear service door. Miraculously, it seemed, no one had observed or heard our escape.

We emerged into an alleyway, where Narmala halted us once more. I glanced around and noted the squalid and filthy rubbish from the hospital lying discarded atop the stones of the pathway. The hospital may have been spotlessly clean, but its environs were putrid. I heard the faint nicker of a horse or pony nearby.

'Ruth. We need to take the bottom of the sheet again,' whispered an obviously tense Narmala.

Ruth did as directed, and I felt myself raised up again, then gently swung forward to rest on what I thought to be a wooden platform sitting at a slight angle.

'The rest of you, into the tray, and lie flat. Do not make a move or a sound from now on,' ordered Narmala briskly.

The others quickly bundled themselves onto the tray of what I now realised was a small cart. We settled down as best we could, either beside, over or across each other. Ruth managed to get by me, so I did not mind the crowded discomfort, even with Kali's garlic-laden bad breath on my other side.

What little light there had been disappeared as a coarse blanket of sacking was thrown over our huddled bodies. I hoped it hadn't been picked up from the rubbish lying in the alleyway.

Narmala whispered to someone else, and I realised that she must've had an accomplice waiting outside to drive the get-away cart. I heard the low click of a tongue, the gentle flick of reins, and the slow clopping of a horse's hooves, along with the gentle creaking of an overloaded cart as we slowly moved off.

I did a brief calculation in my head and realised that from the moment everyone entered my room to this moment at the rear of the hospital, less time had passed than it takes to boil an average-sized kettle.

5

None of us dared make a noise as our horse and cart slowly clipped, clopped and creaked their way through the darkened thoroughfares of Anhilwara Patan. It was still the dead of night, and from the absence of any background noises, it did not sound as if there were any people about on the streets. Time seemed to drag as we wondered where we were heading. From the snatched whispers we shared in the back of the tray, none of us knew more than what Narmala had offered in my bedroom, which was that the queen, Naiki Devi, wanted us dead.

The question in all of our minds must have been – why?

Eventually, the cart came to a stop, and the sacking covering us was hastily whipped away and discarded by Narmala. There was enough starlight filtering through the clouds for me to realise where we were. We were at the 'Queen's Stepwell', the Rani ki Vav, the exquisitely carved and ornamented temple that led to the city's water supply far below the ground. I remembered commenting upon it when we passed by on our entrance into the capital weeks earlier.

Narmala was quick to organise the others, and once again, she, Caspar, Raymond, and Ruth took the corners of the sheet. They then lifted and manoeuvred me off the back of the tray. After some quiet grunts of exertion, they laid me gently upon the dirt and stones of the entrance to the well. My friends tried to be as gentle as they could, but coming down from the tray was much more painful than being placed upon it. I tried not to make any sound, despite the pain burning its way down the length of my body as my scar tissues were stretched to their limit.

'Kamala. The torches,' hissed Narmala, in a quiet but urgent voice. 'Dismantle the tray and bring the reins. Then get rid of the cart and the horse.'

In a few moments, Kamala, a tall and muscled female soldier, produced a sled arrangement from three of the tray boards. She then lashed reins at front and rear of the boards before leading the horse and what remained of the cart away.

Narmala gestured sharply to Raymond and Caspar. 'Help Ippolito onto the tray. Raymond, take the front reins to steer. Caspar, you're the strongest. You can push the tray from the rear. I will explain more as soon as we are out of sight. Follow me and make as little noise as possible.'

In silence, my companions scurried to slide the sled across the short distance of the forecourt and immediately descended into the well a few feet below ground level. Narmala halted our party, using her tinderbox to light one of the six torches Kamala had brought. She handed it to Kali with the instruction, 'Hold it high to light your way and for Raymond and Caspar to also see by. Ruth and Hadar, follow behind them. I'll stay behind to guard our rear. Stop when you reach the landing on the first level down. I will rejoin you there shortly.'

With that, she drew her sword and silently disappeared back up into the darkness.

We made our torchlit way down steps that had been worn smooth and precarious from the thousands of feet that went up and down them every day. Spilled water still lay over some, making them even more slippery and hazardous. Added to this was the steepness of the stepwell, which caused me to be constantly sliding down the wooden tray.

'Grab the bedhead and hang on to it.' Raymond chuckled.

Just as we reached the first landing, I allowed myself to slip a bit further down and managed to kick Raymond in the arse as best I could.

Once we had all arrived, we settled down to wait for Narmala.

'I wish I knew exactly what was going on,' commented Hadar. 'One moment, Kali, Raymond and I are lying asleep. Then Narmala bursts into our room, telling us to get some clothes on and quickly pack a few belongings. She said there was no time to explain, and a few minutes later, she was repeating the performance in Ruth and Ippolito's room.'

'But why would the queen want us dead? We helped her win her battle against the armies of Mohammed of Ghor,' exclaimed Ruth, her forehead furrowed.

Just then, we heard the clatter of sandals on the stone steps above our position, before a breathless Narmala stepped into our small circle of torchlight.

'Come, we must not linger. I will explain as we go down the well.'

The rest of our group got to their feet and followed Narmala, who had taken the torch from Kali. Raymond and Caspar swapped ends on my makeshift stretcher to relieve the tension in their muscles. As we wended our way down the smooth, wet and treacherous steps, Narmala commenced her story.

'Our queen is an amazing, intelligent, caring and loving woman to all of her people. Even more so to those she respects. She has kept the people fed during times of drought and famine. She provides free healthcare and education for the poor and disabled. She usually leads her army from the front and is respected and admired by all who serve under her. She is able to see solutions to problems that have confounded her courtiers and advisors. She is kind and generous to those who support her, always rewarding them and their families for their loyalty and hard work. I truly love her as my queen, as do the people of the kingdom of Gujarat. There are many who would lay down their lives for her.'

Narmala paused, appearing to brace herself for what she had to say next.

'Yet, from time to time, she is plagued by demons. These demons feed her with doubts and fears, so much so that her thinking can become quite fretful and illogical. At times, she will even imagine people and spirits that compel her to do things she would not normally do. Sooner or later, she will become so distressed by all of this that she will even resort to self-harm. This is when the physicians and healers are able to approach her and induce her to take the poppy in such high doses that she becomes immobilised and will often sleep for days on end. After some weeks of this treatment, she will regain her old self and the demons will have deserted her, no longer to trouble her until their next visitation.'

Narmala sighed.

'I learned that the queen was again being haunted by these demons of lies and deception from Kamala this evening, when she was finally able to inform me that it was she, under the queen's specific orders and direct observation, who had skilfully placed the scorpion in your room, just underneath the mattress of your bed. As I said, I was unaware of all of this until earlier this evening.

'And the reason? The queen believes that Ruth and Ippolito really are the blue and red demons and are out to kill her and take little Mularaj away. Naturally, she considers Hadar, Kali, Caspar and Raymond to be lesser demons who are in service to Ruth and Ippolito. I know it all sounds crazy, but right now, so is the queen.

'Shortly before dawn, Kamala will be leading an execution squad to your rooms. They will find that through some demonic agency, the six of you have mysteriously disappeared. We were fortunate that, as far as I know, we were never seen in our escape from the hospital. The queen will no doubt order that an extensive search be undertaken of the hospital and city just in case you demons are still about. She will also order the horse guards to range over the local area. I must be back in time to lead them out.'

'Why did Kamala tell you about the scorpion?' asked Ruth.

'You and I were the subject of much gossip and speculation amongst the women of the queen's horse guard. It was Kamala who suggested we do our elephant battle training with Ganesha over the uneven ground, away from the war encampment, so that we could have some privacy away from prying eyes.'

'She must be very loyal to you,' said Ruth quietly.

A small smile creased the corner of Narmala's mouth.

6

It was another half an hour or more before we reached the seventh and lowest level of the Queen's Stepwell. My incapacitation slowed us down a great deal. We reached the bottom level just as Narmala's leading torchlight was about to splutter itself out, and we had to light the second of the six torches. By the new torch's fresh and crisp light, I was able to see that directly opposite the last step of the well was a metal grill gate set flat into the floor. A few yards away from it was the deep well from which the locals drew their water.

'I have saved the worst of your news till last,' said Narmala. 'First, we must shift this grill. There will be a ladder below. At the bottom, you will find yourself at the opening of a tunnel, which is about twenty miles long and leads to the bottom of a shallow well in the village of Sidhpur to the north of here. It was dug over a hundred years ago as a bolt hole for the royal court, should Anhilwara Patan ever be defeated and invaded. This has never happened, and consequently, the tunnel has fallen into disrepair and disuse. I do not know what condition it is in or what may be down there, but it is where I must leave you. I'm sorry I cannot offer more. If I don't return to the court very soon, the queen, in her demonia, will suspect both me and Kamala of disloyalty and treachery. You have seen some of the ways to die at the queen's whims and will. Her demons can make them even worse.'

I shivered, recalling the deaths of the ranter, the spies and the traitors I had witnessed in the elephant execution pen prior to the battle of Gadaraghatta.

'My last act for you, once you have descended into the tunnel, will be to dislodge some of the stones down here. It will appear like normal subsidence of the underground tunnel, and hopefully will put an end to any immediate pursuit that may be coming your way.'

Caspar withdrew his sword, placed the blade between two bars of the grill, and prised it up from its stony bed. Raymond was quick to grab the edge, and between them, they levered it up and away from the hole. As Narmala had said, there was the ladder leading down into blackness.

'Narmala. On behalf of all of us, thank you for everything you have done for us this night. You have saved our lives,' said Hadar.

Ruth threw her arms around Narmala, and they held each other for a long moment. I noticed tears welling in both their eyes as they parted. I was pleased I felt no pangs of jealousy at this emotional show of affection.

Raymond, holding the torch, was the first to descend. He held the torch high to light the way down for the rest of us. Caspar and Kali helped me unsteadily to my feet, where, despite the pain of stretching the scar tissue across my chest, I placed my arms around Caspar's neck, and he carefully descended the ladder with me hanging from his shoulders. Raymond stood ready to break my fall should I slip. Fortunately, there was no need for the precaution, and Caspar and I made it safely to the bottom. Kali handed down the makeshift stretcher and the others quickly followed.

The tunnel had been hacked and hewed out of rock, giving it a feeling of solidity and safety. The floor had been worn smooth by the passage of water and in most parts could accommodate three or four of us walking comfortably abreast.

With Ruth's assistance, I lowered myself down onto the makeshift stretcher, which was picked up almost immediately by Raymond and Caspar, and we headed off along the tunnel, led by the light of Kali's torch. Ruth called back to Narmala that we were away from the tunnel entrance. Only a few minutes later, we heard the first stone fall and knew Narmala was sealing the entrance.

'We're lucky that this seems to be a straight, flat and even route,' said Kali. 'With luck, and if we push ourselves, we may reach Sidhpur this evening or early tonight. Twenty miles will be a long way, but we have a very early start. I suspect it is still night-time.'

'Let us pray so,' replied Hadar. 'I don't fancy spending more time than we have to down here. Who knows what creatures may lurk in the dark?'

We may have been the only humans in the tunnel, but I soon learned there was plenty of life underground. By the light of the torch, and from my reclined position, I was able to observe the vast, thick blanket of spider webs covering the roof. Along the sides, which seemed to be coated in moss or slimy algae, I frequently caught sight of different types of frogs clinging with their suctioned feet to the walls. Many of them were missing the large eyes that usually characterised their species' unique features. I supposed that in the darkness, they had no need of eyes, and used other senses to make their way in the black night of this underground world. Similarly, I glimpsed one or two very pale snakes, or large worms, that also lacked eyes. Bats had even found their way this far down the tunnel and would occasionally startle us as they flew too close to someone's face or head.

About two hours later, the second torch began to splutter, and we had to light the third, leaving only three more to complete the journey. It would be a close thing to maintain our light for the entire passage. As Raymond and Caspar picked up my stretcher, the middle board snapped in half, depositing me with a painful thump on the floor of the tunnel, and rendering the stretcher useless, as I could not lie upon the remaining two boards without rolling off it.

'That's torn it,' said Raymond. 'How do we get Ippy out of here now?'

'We carry him, like I did down the ladder,' replied Caspar.

'I have a better idea,' said Hadar. 'There's enough of the poppy left in my pack to dull Ippolito's pain when he has to move his right leg. If you both place your arms across his shoulders and he across yours, and then tie his right ankle to one of your own, together the three of you will be able to move much like children in a three-legged race. We should all be able to move along more quickly.'

Caspar knelt down in the watery tunnel and fastened my ankle to Raymond's with the left-over reins from the stretcher.

It was an excellent idea, and after the poppy had infused its way into my brain and body, I found the sensation of being propelled along by others somewhat euphoric. I felt we were making very good time. Ruth kept up the same 'one, two, one, two' tempo that Narmala had used on the hospital stairs, and we progressed in an even and almost uneventful gait for the next few hours.

In my euphoric state, I imagined we had become some oversized cave creature scuttling its five-legged way along the tunnel. Unfortunately, the poppy also affected my gait, and on two occasions I stumbled, causing the three of us to fall to the floor with multiple scrapes and bruises. With the help of the others, we were quickly back on our feet and scuttling our way along the passage once again.

The third torch began to flicker and fade, and we lit our fourth, leaving just two more to complete our journey. The fourth torch did not burn as brightly as the others, and within an hour, it too was dying, requiring us to light our second-last torch.

'We must hurry,' said Kali with some urgency, 'or we will be spending the rest of this journey in darkness, and I do not fancy that prospect.'

'Wait. What is that sound?' said Ruth. She had the most acute hearing of all of us, and we stopped talking and moving.

'There it is again,' she said.

Suddenly, I heard it. Off in the distance ahead was a faint, high-pitched chittering sound, and it was coming closer.

'Oh, Shiva's shit,' exclaimed Kali. 'Rats.'

'And lots of them, by the sound,' added Raymond.

'Quickly. Huddle as closely together as you possibly can,' ordered Caspar, all action and no panic. Unlike the rest of us. 'Kali, come here and take Ippolito's arm. Give me the torch.'

Caspar took the lead, holding the torch lower than Kali had before. It was then I saw why he had grabbed the lead and the torch. He was the only one amongst us wearing boots and not sandals. Despite being huddled together, we moved faster, and I concentrated as hard as I could on listening to Ruth's gentle and steady tempo, moving my legs with Raymond and Kali and working on keeping my balance.

It was only a short time before we saw them. Dozens and dozens of yellow eyes reflecting the torchlight were spread across the width of the tunnel ahead of us.

'Just keep as close as you can behind me,' said Caspar as he drew his broadsword. He moved off at a steady pace and began waving the torch and his sword around in front of him. The rats seemed unafraid of him at first, but as we came closer, most of them parted away to the side. A few were bolder than the others and ran toward us in attack, their front teeth showing viciously in the torchlight. Caspar was a whirlwind of action, slashing at them with his sword, burning and singeing with the torch and on several occasions launching them high with well-aimed kicks.

'Keep going,' ordered Caspar, 'and keep together. I think they're starting to hesitate.'

He continued his wild swinging of torch and blade and even started to yell and make all sorts of fearsome noises. We joined him in a squalling, screaming and screeching chorus. All of this seemed to work in either terrorising or confusing the rats, as none of them came close enough to bite us, and they moved to the walls of the tunnel as we progressed down its middle. None followed us, either.

Time seemed to drag as we made our way along the passage, but the number of rats ahead and around us began to dwindle, and finally, we were past the vile swarm of filthy little beasts. We could hear them chittering away as we continued on down the corridor, and eventually, their noise disappeared altogether.

Time passed, and the fifth torch began its spluttering demise. We lit our sixth and final torch. I noticed that the scattered puddles beneath our feet had become larger and were spreading out to cover the entire floor of the passage. They were still shallow enough not to impede our progress. However, as we went along, the water gradually rose to our ankles and did begin to slow us down.

Another hour later, we were wading through waist-high water when Kali pointed ahead, to where a faint shimmer of orange light across the surface of the water suggested we were drawing near to the tunnel's end. Hopefully, we would soon emerge into the evening light from the village well of Sidhpur.

The faint shimmer, however, also revealed a sinuous pair of ridges trailing a pair of large yellow eyes, which were slowly swimming their way toward our party.

'Crocodile!' shrieked Kali.

7

'Ruth. Kali. Behind us, quickly,' snapped Caspar. 'Raymond. Draw your sword and cut Ipp's leg ties.'

Raymond quickly slashed the ties about our ankles, but as they were no longer helping to support me, I tumbled back into the water. The crocodile lunged in my direction. I surfaced to see both Caspar's long sword and Raymond's shorter falchion come down upon the monster's head and neck. This only enraged the beast further, but did slow its attack in my direction, as it turned to face its two unexpected adversaries.

Casper managed to yell, 'Kali, keep the torch high so we can see!' as he and Raymond continued to rain blows on the leathery skin. Their efforts were holding it at bay, but it was becoming more aggressive in its thrashings and lunges. Its wounds were only shallow and barely bleeding. I felt arms under my shoulders and realised Hadar and Ruth were dragging me away from the flashing swords and gnashing teeth, allowing Caspar and Raymond greater freedom to attack the loudly roaring beast.

Out of the corner of my eye, I noticed Ruth's arm flick forward. The reflected torchlight in one of the crocodile's eyes suddenly went out, and the monster thrashed wildly in a new pain. This was followed by a long, growling howl from deep in its throat. The beast leapt from the water and lunged at Caspar, causing him to stumble backwards and fall into the water, losing his sword under the surface.

The great jaws opened wide and were about to clamp down on Caspar's legs when Raymond did one of the bravest things I have ever seen. With his short falchion raised vertically, he dived at the creature's mouth, placing his forearm and sword within just as the great jaws were slammed shut with a powerful force. The point of the upright blade was driven through the roof of the beast's mouth and emerged from its snout. The sword's metal crosspiece was jammed between its razor-sharp teeth, allowing Raymond to quickly withdraw his hand, albeit minus some small strips of flesh.

The crocodile issued a gargled roar of rage. Caspar had retrieved his sword and now stood facing the crocodile on his own.

'Draw him to the left,' called Ruth.

Caspar did so, and immediately, one of Ruth's sharp little throwing knives lodged in the crocodile's other eye. The beast was now blinded, its lethal gnashing jaw significantly disabled by Raymond's falchion still sticking up from its snout. The fight had turned to their advantage, as the pain-racked animal flicked and turned, desperately trying to escape. In one wide, sweeping blow, Raymond severed a foreleg, quickly followed by its rear leg on the same side. Like a crippled spider, the crocodile kept turning in circles, allowing Caspar to rain repeated blows on the back of its head and neck. The beast thrashed wildly in a frothing pink spray of blood and water. Eventually, it bled out and lay dead and still, its head half severed, its mouth a ruin and two slender knives protruding from its eye sockets.

Ruth waded over to the dead beast and calmly retrieved her knives.

'Let's get out of here,' ordered a breathless Caspar.

None of us were slow to oblige, and within half an hour, we emerged from the entrance to the well of Sidhpur just as the last torch spluttered out.

It was just on sunset, and a crowd of people stood around the entrance to the well, cheering us as welcome heroes. They had been aware of the fierce struggle going on in the well, as the sound had travelled to them along the tunnel. None of them had been willing to enter it, as they had no idea what was happening within. As it turned out, the crocodile had moved into the well some weeks prior and had seen the deaths of two women and a child of the village during its short tenancy. The people were rightly afraid of it.

We were feted by the villagers that night. Kali was almost talked hoarse, as he had to translate just about everything that was said to us and everything we said. The food was simple but flavoursome, and throughout the long day with all its excitement and adventure, from the moment Narmala had burst into our rooms to our emergence from the tunnel, we had not eaten, and so we dug into our food ravenously and with relish.

At one point, using Kali as translator, Caspar arose and related the story of Raymond's bravery in placing his hand and shortsword in the crocodile's mouth. He proposed a toast to the heroism of his brother in arms. As one, the villagers stood and applauded Raymond. Raymond was gracious in his acceptance of this praise, particularly from a knight he clearly admired, and cheekily waved his bandaged and somewhat bloodied hand to the crowd around us. He was a little bit high on praise and poppy – the latter courtesy of Hadar.

We were eventually shown to a well-appointed guests' bungalow, where we were able to take a well-earned rest. We all fell asleep almost immediately. None of us woke till the next morning was well advanced. As I stepped outside with Caspar and Ruth assisting me, we noticed that the men of the village had been down the well and had dragged the crocodile out with ropes. I looked at the monster in the clear light of day and realised it was more than twelve feet long, its great snout and jaw accounting for almost three feet.

The ropes were removed, and the women of the village set about with very sharp knives and hatchets to cut and distribute the meat, organs and other useful products. Their first act was to open the mouth wide, slice and remove the tongue and retrieve Raymond's falchion, which they cleaned and presented to him with great reverence and friendly pats upon his shoulders. With many blows from a hatchet, the women then removed the five to six-foot tail from the reptile's body. They skinned it and began cutting the pale flesh into slices, probably to make crocodile steaks, stews or curries. The body was turned over, and the softer underbelly was quickly slit open to spill its contents to the ground. The heart, liver, kidneys and some other organs were severed and removed, presumably for the cooking pot as well.

While this was happening, others were busy skinning the tough hide from the beast's back and sides. This, I learned, would be carefully cut, dried, cured and shaped into a unique suit of body armour. The claws and teeth would be cleansed and used as either personal or household ornamentation. There was no longer any use for either of its punctured eyes. Apparently, an intact eye could be skilfully filled with a gum that hardened the orb. These were worn as a personal decoration and used for warding off undesirable spirits and demons.

There was something deeply satisfying in watching this dissection, the final end of the monster that had terrorised all of us more than we had ever been before – and that included by assassin and shark attacks! I was looking forward to a crocodile steak as a final act of revenge.

Later in the morning, I was concerned when Hadar emerged from our bungalow. He looked more haggard and simply worn out than I had seen him to date, and I said so.

'Thank you for your concern, Ippolito. You see into me as a healer would. I believe a couple of days to rest, recover and recuperate are in order. The well is now safe, and if agents from the queen are seen, we can quickly hide down there. Besides, we need to make plans now that everything has been turned on its head.'

Raymond nodded his agreement to Hadar's proposal. He was enjoying the attention due a hero from some of the younger women of the village, who seemed to be fawning, some quite jealously, over him.

And he liked it.

8

Indeed, Raymond did not return to our bungalow that night, or the next, or the next. None of us begrudged his youthful inclinations in the light of what had happened in the tunnel and his willingness to sacrifice at least a hand for the sake of his comrade in arms. In fact, Caspar frequently smiled at Raymond's furtive return to our premises each morning. He, too, was no doubt thinking of the beautiful Isabella back in Outremer.

'He is still only a squire and has not taken any knightly vows of poverty or chastity. I see no problem in his enjoying himself for a while,' commented Caspar, upon hearing Hadar and Kali chuckling about the joys of youth.

Ruth and I, too, had made opportunities to be together and pursue our own enthusiasms. Hadar and Kali no doubt chuckled over the joys of our youth as well.

We still, however, had to be about the business of our quest, and it was on our third day in the village that Hadar called us to a meeting.

'Well,' said Hadar, once we were seated in our bungalow, 'the simple question is, where to from here? Any thoughts at all would be welcome.'

Caspar was first to speak. 'Logistically, going west and south is out of the question until we receive news that the queen is dispossessed of her demons. Even then, I believe it may not be safe to go that way. The queen has shown she has a capricious nature even when not affected by her demons.

'The north is also closed to us. The villagers tell me that the country is being overrun by Mohammed of Ghor's allies, the Turushkas, and other Turkish tribes. They are pursuing a policy of conquest, terror and scorched earth throughout those lands. We would not be safe at all.'

'Speaking for myself,' said Ruth, 'I would prefer not to return to the south with its heat, humidity, poverty and disease. I actually feel safer and more comfortable here.'

'We are still too close to Naiki Devi in this village,' said Hadar. 'We do not know if there are search parties heading in this direction or not. I'm sure Narmala would try to put her party off our trail, but there will be others keen to please the queen. We have to move on. Do we still make Kashmir our destination, as planned prior to the news of Baldwin's death, or not?'

'Kali speaks highly of the beauty of his country,' I said, 'and once properly back on my feet, I would like to see it. Also, I am intrigued by what we might learn from these supposed holy men of the Himalayas, particularly in the way of healing practices.'

Ruth agreed with a definite 'Me too.'

'Raymond. What say you?' said Hadar, looking directly at him.

'Simple, really. I go where you go,' he said, and gave that cheeky smile of his.

'Kashmir, then?' posed Hadar.

'Kashmir,' was the unanimous agreement.

'Oh, joy,' sighed Kali, 'I'm going home.'

***

Over the next two days, we put together our kits and supplies as best we could. They had been extensively depleted in our hurried and unexpected escape from Anhilwara Patan. The villagers were exceedingly generous, providing us with food, clothing, utensils, light shelter materials, and a high-sided pack sled. An animal to haul the sled would have been useful, but there were none available in the village. Hadar even managed to renew his supply of poppy from a local healer, along with other herbal ingredients he said could come in helpful.

On the morning of our departure, the whole village turned out to bid us farewell. In the midst of all the well-wishes, hugs, handshakes and, for Raymond at least, lingering kisses, a small group of women approached bearing yet more gifts. To Raymond and Caspar, they presented silver warrior's armbands, and to Ruth, a necklace. All were made or inlaid with the teeth and claws of the crocodile the three had collectively killed, which had been meticulously cleaned and bleached. Their whiteness gleamed in the sun, along with the silver bedding of the armbands. They looked good on Caspar and Raymond's upper arms, as did Ruth's necklace, resting on her bodice.

We said our final farewells and set off into the east, then to the north. Raymond, Kali, and Caspar took turns in hauling the sled and arranged to swap over every mile or so to keep fresh, should we need to make a run from pursuit. I had begun recovering much more quickly during the last two days and was able to offer short periods of assistance with this task.

Our journey to and through the foothills of Kashmir was by and large uneventful. The scenery was astounding, the creeks and rivers full of the sweetest water, the wildlife plentiful, the locals friendly and inviting. It was the perfect healing for my body; plenty of gentle exercise, along with the massages and Raymond's daily torture sessions, had me back in good physical health and strength within a month. The scar would always limit some movements, but it was not long before I resumed my sword training with Caspar and Raymond and found myself back on a competitive footing – with Raymond, at least.

As we hiked along, Ruth and I resumed our morning lessons with Hadar. Our enthusiasm was renewed after the interruption our learning had received thanks to Mohammed of Ghor's war upon Naiki Devi and Gujarat. Ruth had many questions based upon what she had seen of my body in its most exposed state and throughout the healing process. Hadar explained many of the structures she had glimpsed beneath my skin. She was most intrigued to understand the reason for the heat she said had radiated from me in times of infection and during the early stages of the wound's healing. Hadar was of the belief that it was related to increased blood flow, either to enrich the healing tissue with as many nutrients as possible or to fight off the humours of infection.

Kali was a great source of information as we travelled, naming prominent mountains, rivers and other significant landmarks, which he often coloured with stories of local heroes and legends. In between sightseeing, he provided us with further lessons in the local dialects and languages of northern Hind as well as the customs and manners of the population.

As we travelled along in those mild weeks of spring, it was impossible not to notice the high range of snow-capped mountains rising in the far north-east. Each day, we walked closer toward them, but they never seemed to get nearer, only higher. I happened to look back rather than forward one afternoon and noticed a cloud of dust behind us to the west. It was still many miles away, but I immediately pointed it out to Caspar.

'It's a horse troop, alright,' observed Caspar. 'A herd of wild animals make a different sort of dust cloud. That one is from horses riding in a line. It would seem the queen has not given up on chasing down her two precious demons.'

He shaded his eyes with his hand to break down the obscuring glare of the day.

'They don't appear to be following our trail directly, but I think they may be travelling a parallel path. If they decide to cut across country, we could easily be discovered.'

He turned slowly around, scrutinising the terrain as he did so.

'From now on, we must avoid the open grassland and keep to the forested part of the countryside. It will slow us down somewhat but will help keep us hidden. Let us pray they have no outriders or scouts this far from their line. I'm afraid this is going to mean no fires and cold food and drink until we are sure we're well away from them or they turn back.'

'Oh, joy,' muttered Raymond.

'Raymond, I'm making you responsible for keeping a regular eye on their progress,' said Caspar. 'Let me know if there is any change in their direction, and if they stop, slow down or appear to put on speed. Check behind you every few minutes. Time will be a critical factor if we have to run for it.'

Our journey through the forests took us higher and higher into the foothills leading up to the mountains of northern Hind. We passed by and through beautiful tree-lined valleys adorned with flowers of every shape and colour, bubbling and burbling brooks that teemed with fish, and deep, dark forested areas where the trees seemed to reach the sky and blanket all sunlight below. And, always in front of us, getting higher and higher as we approached them, were the snow-capped mountains of the Himalayas.

After three days, there was no longer any sign of pursuit. No dust clouds hung in the air to the north or west. Presumably, the horse guards had given up the chase and turned back. We all fervently hoped so.

After we had crested a ridge, we looked down into a very pretty valley. A gurgling little river ran in small cascades and falls of only a foot or two. Stone fords and wooden walkways bridged the stream at different places as it flowed past a small village. On one side of the river were neat rows of vegetable crops, while on the other side were clustered various peasants', farmers' and artisans' huts. There appeared to be a small marketplace, along with a larger building I took to be a temple dedicated to one of the many gods of the region.

'What is this pretty little village named?' asked Ruth of Kali.

At first, Kali remained mute. Then he turned toward us, a tear welling in the corner of one of his eyes, and slowly said, 'It is my home. It has no name.'

9

As we descended toward Kali's village, I could not help but note that there was a lack of the activity one would normally see in a rural village toward the middle of the day. Few women attended laundry or washed cooking utensils in the river, nor were any children splashing and playing around their mothers. Only a handful of peasants worked in the fields, and smoke rose from barely a half dozen fires, where one would expect a cooking pot in front of almost every hut at this time of day. Those who were about the village appeared slow and lethargic as they moved between huts or through the fields. From some of the huts, I could hear children sobbing as if in pain. A middle-aged woman sitting by one of the few fires was holding her stomach with both hands and slowly rocking back and forth.

'There is something amiss in this village,' declared Hadar, signalling a halt. 'I suspect that some illness unknown to me is afoot. It would be wise to cover your faces, and do not touch anyone or their personal objects till we have some idea of what we are up against.'

We entered the village and made our way over to the woman rocking herself by a cooking fire. As we approached, she held her hand up to warn us away.

'Keep your distance, strangers, and pass through quickly. There is illness here, and death has been visited upon some of our children.'

'We are physicians, healers and helpers,' said Hadar, with a few verbal prompts from Kali. 'We may be able to offer comfort or advice to you. Can you tell me when and how this illness came about?'

'It started with the children about nine months ago,' began the woman, still holding her stomach. 'At first, only a few fell ill. They all had the watery flux, and many suffered with swollen bellies.'

The woman's eyes took on a faraway aspect before she continued. 'Then many came down with a sore throat, a wheezing cough and a high fever. The cough was terrible to hear, and they produced so much fluid from their lungs at night that they nearly choked.'

I noticed a small tear appear in the corner of her eye.

'All this time, the flux continued, and their bellies became even more swollen and painful. Most could only tolerate small amounts of fluid without vomiting everything up again. It was less than a month before the first of the children started dying.'

Another tear appeared to join the first as it trailed down her cheek.

'Gradually, more children, and then adults, started to become ill with the same symptoms. Some of the adults developed other symptoms as well. The yellow disease of the skin and eyes was the most common. For others, the watery flux soon turned into bloody, and before long, they too died. Nearly half the village has died or left to try and escape the disease. There are no babies, and only a handful of children are still alive.'

'Thank you, er, madam. What is your name?' asked Hadar politely.

'I am known as Mindi,' she replied.

Suddenly, Kali became very animated, and stated more than asked, 'Daughter of Sari and Maraka.'

'Why, yes,' replied Mindi.

'Sister! It is I. Your brother, Kali.' He went to step forward and embrace her, but Hadar held him back. 'Hadar, let me go. This is my youngest sister!'

'Your only sister, and your only sibling now,' said Mindi, bowing her head in grief.

Kali looked as though a knife had just torn through his heart.

'Mindi,' said Hadar, turning back to her, 'until I can identify and treat this illness, you must tell everyone in the village to keep their distance from our group. We are going to withdraw and make our camp outside the village perimeter. In the meantime, make sure that all your drinking water is boiled before consumption. Added to this, I would request that every man, woman and child deliver their first stool of the day to a place nearby, where my colleagues and I may examine it.'

Mindi appeared to understand this. She looked to Kali and blew a kiss, then turned to take the message to the villagers. We moved away from the cooking fire and retraced our steps to about a hundred yards from the last house in the village, where we set up our meagre camp. Once we were settled and our evening meal was simmering over the fire, Hadar commenced a review of what we had learned so far of the disease afflicting the village.

'So,' said Hadar, looking at Ruth and me, sitting by the fire, 'what are the presenting foci of this disease?'

'Gastrointestinal, respiratory and, given the yellowing of eyes and skin, hepatic as well,' I answered.

'The nocturnal coughing and choking on fluids suggest an upper respiratory focus,' added Ruth, 'as the children were obviously able to cough it up. If it were located purely in the lungs, the children would've been less able to expel their secretions.'

'Good point,' replied Hadar. 'That accounts for the wheezing breath sounds as well.'

'The watery flux becoming bloody suggests that there is trauma occurring in the bowels,' I said. 'Could it be that some agent is present in the bowel and causing this damage even in other organs?'

'I have long believed in the seen and unseen agents of human trauma and disease,' replied Hadar, 'and I believe you may be correct. We must rely on our senses for this, my young apprentices. Tomorrow, you will have to use the sense of sight to look for signs of infestation or infection in the stools presented to us. You will have to use your nose to detect subtleties in intensity and nature of odour, and to some degree touch, albeit with a spatula of some kind.'

I smiled at Ruth, trying to hide my amusement. 'I've had many weeks of tuition in the matters of stool appreciation.'

I managed a sly wink in Caspar and Kali's direction.

'It would be very unworthy of me to keep this knowledge to myself when your expertise in this aspect of healing is somewhat bereft of a similar experience.'

Caspar and Kali were openly smiling at this relegation, and I fell off my log in mirth at the look on Ruth's face.

Ruth immediately sat on my chest, gently holding me down, and said, 'Do you remember your question to Hadar about the taste test? That, my love, is all yours.'

10

From early to mid-morning the next day, the villagers brought their 'first offerings' to a trestle arrangement they had rigged the evening before a short distance from our camp. Beside it, Hadar had placed an empty bucket, and upon it were laid several wooden spatulas he and Raymond had whittled the night before. Most of the offerings were transported upon the large leaves of a plant that grew in plentiful patches around the village. Other offerings, due to their fluid nature, had been collected in rough wooden bowls.

Hadar, Ruth and I stood before the table, trying to ignore the odour of the specimens before us. Raymond stood nearby, interested to observe, but staying his hand and nose when it came to the examinations.

'A healthy human stool is usually softly formed and has a general uniformity in colour and texture,' directed Hadar. 'This, of course, varies with diet and intake. Cast your eyes over what is before you and seek out anything that does not conform with the rest of the stool.'

'Obviously, this one is streaked with very dark and dull red lines. I suspect it is old blood, probably from high in the bowel,' offered Ruth.

'And this one has the bright red streaks of a recent and lower bleed,' I added.

'I would say, on a casual examination, that about half these stools show evidence of intestinal bleeding,' declared Hadar. 'Now I want you to take a straight-edge spatula and spread the bloody specimens flat across the leaf.'

We did so, and both of us were startled by what was revealed. Both samples contained a wriggling white worm about fourteen inches long. A quick smear of the other stools revealed yet more of these worms, sometimes more than one to a sample.

'Thus, we have our culprit,' said a very satisfied Hadar, poking one of the worms with a probe to turn it over. 'Although I have to admit that these intestinal worms are somewhat larger and thicker than those a physician would normally see in day-to-day practice. This probably accounts for the greater mortality amongst the villagers.'

I could tell by the look on her face Ruth was as nauseated as I was at the notion of these fat, white, wriggling worms making their way around a person's interior.

'Now I want you to use these hooked probes to place these worms in the empty bucket, then cover it over.'

This was harder than it sounds, as the little beggars constantly wriggled and writhed and fell off the hook. By mid-morning, we had the bucket a quarter full of twisting and turning intestinal worms. It revolted all of us. Hadar made a point of showing the contents to the headman of the village and a number of other village elders, all of whom reacted with horror. It helped bring home the need for treatment. With the headman and elders' encouragement, the villagers would be more receptive to what Hadar had in mind.

'So, my young friends. What do you recall of the treatments for intestinal worms?' questioned Hadar of the both of us.

'There are many,' I said. 'Wormwood, hellebore, camphor, senna, to name a few. The question is, do they grow in these parts of the world?'

'Hopefully, Kali, Mindi or some of the other villagers may be able to help out with this one. If only I had my *liber herbalis* with me, we could show them pictures.'

'Provide me with some charcoal and a surface I can draw on and I can solve that problem,' said Ruth.

'Of course,' said Hadar. 'I had forgotten the artistic skills you displayed on our circus cart.'

By mid-afternoon, Ruth had produced almost a dozen detailed sketches of the differing plants that could be used to treat the intestinal worms. The villagers, recognising some of them, set about collecting as many and as much of them as possible.

'I am inclined,' said Hadar, 'to attack this problem on two fronts and to keep the assault up for a number of days, to ensure the maximum eradication and expulsion of these worms.'

'Would that be both oral infusions and enemata over a period of, say, a week?' I offered.

'Correct. Infusions in the evening and an enema to start the day.'

* * *

I will not dwell upon the effect Hadar's treatment regime had on the villagers. It was a case of the cure being almost as bad as the poison, and it was a very messy matter. Ruth and I definitely became sick and tired of administering enemas morning in and morning out. Ruth attended the women and the few remaining children, and I the men.

Suffice to say, a fortnight later, a new energy and vigour surrounded the village. The farmers returned to the fields, the artisans to their workshops; the cooking fires were all alight, and the remaining children of the village played happily outside and inside family huts and bungalows.

Hadar had one more injunction to impart to the villagers, and that was to cease the practice of using their own excrement as fertiliser for their crops and fields. This was only serving to perpetuate the worm infestations year after year.

Ruth and I both felt a sense of tremendous satisfaction over our involvement in the transformation of the village. It seemed we had passed yet another milestone in our quest on the road to becoming healers.

Despite this achievement, we knew that we still had many more miles to go. Those miles stretched out in front of us to where the western end of the Himalayas greeted the eastern border of Kashmir.

'Do you suppose Kali's story about the holy men and their secret cache of ancient wisdom and knowledge is true, or are we on a wild goose chase?' I asked Ruth, as we sat and watched the ever-present snow atop the Himalayas changing colours with the setting of the sun.

'I spoke with Mindi, and she too believes that the holy men are custodians of some kind of secret knowledge. She said she has no idea exactly what this might be, but she did mention them seeming to have uncommon powers or skills.'

'Let us hope that we can find them and their monastery as quickly as possible. I don't fancy braving the cold up there in all that snow for too long a time.'

'Mindi seemed confident that Kali had a good idea of how to find their sanctuary,' she replied. 'Before he took up magic tricks, he spent much of his youth exploring the mountains. He hasn't let us down yet.'

'Brrr! All this talk of snow is making me cold,' I said. 'Might be time to cuddle up and get warm again, I think.'

Ruth smiled and poked me in the ribs. 'Is that what you call it?'

11

Two weeks later, we were approaching the snowline of the mountains and passing through a forest that was bursting with colour. The flowering trees, Kali informed us, were called rhododendrons. Their blooms were bigger than a man's fist and came in every shade of pink, red, purple, yellow and white, as well as variegated ones of more than one hue. Ruth made herself a garland of different colours each day we spent in the forest. I thought they looked good on her and said so.

We were clad very differently now. Gone were the lightweight cottons and silks of lowland and southern Hind. The people of Kali's village had provided us with clothing more suitable to the cold of the mountains. All of us wore leather fur-lined leggings, long-sleeved woollen vests and quilted, down-filled overcoats that reached our knees. Added to this were gloves, scarves, heavy boots and fur-lined caps. The village also supplied us with another slightly larger sled, which we took turns in pairs to haul along behind us. It carried our belongings and supplies, as well as a carefully stacked store of wood to use as fuel. Finally, the villagers had provided us with dried meats, vegetables and grains, which could be easily restored and flavoured with a few spices upon being boiled in water. Not the most appetising but warming and filling.

With the exception of Kali, none of us liked the cold mountain air, coming as we did from warmer lowland climes. It seemed that, despite our attire, our feet, hands and faces were always freezing. Each of us seemed to have a permanent drop of moisture hanging, or about to drip, from our noses. Sometimes, the icy air hurt our teeth – that is, when they weren't chattering away so uncontrollably our jaws ached from their constant movement. We were all looking forward to reaching some kind of warmth and shelter.

Kali had informed us that the monastery we were seeking was known as the Buddha's Smile, and stated he was confident he could find the entrance based on childhood recollection and stories.

It was toward the end of our fifth day in the snowfield that the snow leopard attacked. Kali, as usual, was acting as our guide, when from behind an ice mound a black, grey and white blur flashed out, clamping itself to Kali's side, using its claws and teeth to slash and bite at him. Both victim and attacker rolled in the snow, Kali's shrieks accompanied by the leopard's roars and snarls, carried around the slope. Caspar had drawn his sword and was trying to get a cut in on the snow leopard, but the pair were rolling around so much he couldn't do so safely without risking harm to Kali. Finally, his moment came, and he brought his sword down across the leopard's back, crippling the animal. It released its hold on Kali and attempted to get away but was unable to do so on two now-useless back legs. Caspar brought the coup de grace down on its head, and it lay still in the blood and snow.

Miraculously, Kali had got off very lightly. The thickly padded clothes and scarf he was wearing were somewhat shredded, but they had saved his skin from the leopard's claws and teeth. His only injury was a torn left ear, which Ruth and I stitched and patched up with some bandages.

'You must have been born under a very lucky star, Kali,' observed Raymond. 'You were the only one to survive the shark attack at sea, and now you can add being attacked by a snow leopard as well. Very impressive.'

We left the leopard in the snow, not bothering to take what would have been a very valuable and luxurious pelt, and moved on, Kali still volunteering to lead the way. We had not gone more than one hundred yards before Ruth called a sudden halt.

'Do you hear that?' she said.

'No,' and 'What?' came our various replies.

'Sounds like crying. Over there, I think.' She immediately moved in that general direction and disappeared behind a snowdrift.

'Wait,' I called, 'not on your own!' and quickly set off in pursuit with Raymond by my side.

The next thing I heard was a squeal of joy from Ruth and a tiny, sharp hissing sound. I rounded the drift and there, in front of a small, protected cleft in the snow, sat Ruth with a small bundle of grey-and-black-spotted fluff in her hands. She raised it to her face and rubbed the soft pelt against her cheek.

'Oh. She's gorgeous. So cute. Look at the little markings around her eyes, just like kohl! What a beauty she is.'

The kitten was a little over a foot long from tip of nose to tail and stood about six inches high at the shoulders. Her pelt was naturally lighter in colour than her mother's, and she was still very fluffy. She was sleekly proportioned and had a sharp, intelligent look in her eyes. I have to admit, like Ruth, I did think her a real beauty.

It was evident to me that Ruth had very quickly fallen in love with the little creature and would not be giving it up lightly.

'I think we just gained another travelling companion,' observed Raymond. 'I guess the mother was only trying to protect its cub.'

'And that's why I am going to keep it and rear it,' said Ruth with emphasis, raising the ball of fluff to eye level and making a cooing sound before letting it snuggle into the warmth of her neck.

The members of our group reacted differently to the arrival of our new travelling companion. Being young, Raymond, Ruth and I naturally accepted the presence of the kitten as a welcome novelty. Hadar was noncommittal but stressed that a strict regime of training must commence straight away if the animal was not to be a threat or nuisance to anyone. Caspar was against the presence of the kitten as an extra drain on our resources and time. Kali was very much in favour of keeping it, as snow leopards were highly valued as intelligent pets in the royal courts and often roamed freely within a palace, claws and teeth duly blunted by specialist trainers and handlers.

'I think she has been weaned from the teat, as her teeth are developed enough to chew with, and there were no obvious milky dugs on the mother's body,' said Kali. 'You will have to chew her feed to a manageable pulp for a little while yet.'

'No problem,' answered Ruth. 'I'll share my rations with her until she can hunt her own food.'

'So! What do we call her?' asked Raymond.

Ruth thought for a moment, then said, 'I think I'll call her Whisper.'

With that, she pulled the front of her coat out and deposited Whisper into the warmth and scent of her cleavage, where she quickly settled.

I tried not to think about how nice that would be.

12

'I think we're getting nearer to the entrance to the monastery,' Kali informed us two days later. 'Look out for what appears to be the entrance to a snow or ice cave. I believe it is on the other side of that steep rise that lies before us, but I cannot be sure, as it is many years since I, as a boy, visited the monastery. The ever-changing drifts of snow have made it difficult to recognise the features I remember.'

We surveyed the surrounding mountain whiteness, shading our eyes with our hands to reduce the glare.

'You can see the next part of the journey will be dangerous. We'll need to take extra care, as the ridge will probably be covered in ice, not snow. It will be slippery and extremely treacherous.'

I looked up at the steep ascent ahead of us and wondered how we, let alone our supply sled, would make it to the top.

'We'll have to zig-zag back and forth across the slope of the ridge, slowly working our way up,' continued Kali. 'As a safety measure, I would have you each craft a walking stick with a sharpened end, which you can use to stabilise yourself. There should be suitable shafts amongst the wood we have brought.'

An hour later, we had finished whittling points to our walking staves and were preparing to begin the most difficult part of our ascent so far. Kali led the way, followed by Caspar and then Hadar.

Ruth came next, with a capering and frolicking Whisper following in her tracks. Thanks to a little bit of pre-chewed food and warm cleavage, the kitten seemed to have quickly and affectionately bonded with Ruth. Raymond and I brought up the rear, along with the sled, Raymond pulling and I pushing.

We progressed through the morning, making our slow but steady zig-zagging way up the face of the rise. Raymond and I swapped position several times, as pushing the sled through the churned-up snow and ice left by our fellow travellers in front of us was hard work. At one stage, Whisper scampered up to play around my feet, almost tripping me over several times. I eventually picked her up and placed her upon my shoulder, much to her consternation. I felt her sharp little claws pierce my quilted coat as she clung fretfully to the cloth. Within a short time, she got used to the rhythm of my gait and the experience of being too far off the ground and settled down comfortably on my shoulders, front paws hanging forward, rear paws and tail falling across my shoulder blades. From there, I could tell by her gaze that she was able to watch Ruth making her way along the ridge. Every now and then, she would turn her head and lick the side of my face with her raspy pink tongue. I quite liked it, even more so when Ruth looked back at us and laughed.

Suddenly, there was a commotion ahead. Hadar's arms were flailing wildly in circles, his body slowly toppling to the side. Caspar made a desperate lunge to grab hold of his coat – just a moment too late.

At first, Hadar slid down the side of the steep slope, making desperate attempts to slow himself by grabbing at the snow, trying to use the stave he still held, but then he hit an icy part of the slope and his speed accelerated. He careered into a drift and was catapulted into the air, eventually coming to land in a crumpled and unmoving heap on the rock-hard ice, not far from where we had started our ascent earlier in the day.

Ruth's scream of horror rapidly brought Whisper down from

my shoulder to scamper to her side, her fear of heights quickly forgotten in concern for her mistress. Ruth scooped her up.

'Stay calm,' called Caspar. 'We don't need another tragedy.'

'Look,' said Raymond urgently. 'Did he just move his arm? We must get back down to him. Quickly.' None of us needed any further convincing.

Going down was more difficult than going up; we repeatedly had to use our staves to prevent the sliding and slipping that accompanied our momentum downhill. I became aware of Kali urging us to slow down. He yelled out that we could create a snowfall or, worse, an avalanche that might cover Hadar and diminish his chances of survival even further.

Raymond was first to Hadar's side, closely followed by Ruth and me. Caspar and Kali hung back to let us examine Hadar. He was only just conscious and only able to make the barest incoherent mumble. The hard ice had treated him harshly, and it was apparent that bones were broken in each of his now misshapen limbs. His face was bloodied from a possibly broken nose, and there was an ominous purple swelling over his left temple and around the ear.

'Hadar,' I said, 'can you wriggle your toes or move your feet?' Nothing.

I tried again, making sure he was looking directly at me. 'Hadar! It's Ippolito. Can you wriggle your toes for me? Please!'

There was a small movement inside his left boot but none in his right.

'Thank heaven,' offered Ruth, in relief that the spinal column was not severed.

That brief reassurance was ended abruptly when Caspar said, 'Raymond. You and I must climb back up to retrieve the sled to transport Hadar and get the medical supplies he needs, particularly the poppy extract.'

They both left immediately, leaving Ruth, Kali and me to minister to Hadar. Mercifully, Hadar had lapsed into unconsciousness again, which allowed Ruth and me opportunity to gently assess his condition.

'Kali,' I said, 'you know how to assess the heart from the pulse in the neck. Please do so, and don't hesitate to let us know of any changes in his heart rate, rhythm or quality. And watch the rise and fall of his chest to give us some idea of how he is breathing.'

Ruth and I began a careful head-to-toe inspection, taking one side each and working our way down Hadar's body. After half an hour, we were done. Our findings were not good.

The head injury Hadar had sustained to the left temple region was my main concern. There was no telling at this stage what damage to the brain may have occurred. Ruth was equally concerned about a swelling below the left ribs that indicated possible damage to his internal organs. Mercifully, none of his broken ribs appeared to have punctured, or be threatening, his lungs, as there was no frothing of the blood in and around his mouth. The list of broken bones was a long one: nose, left collarbone, possible left hip, unknown number of ribs, both long bones of the upper arms, both long bones of the upper legs and the lower ones of the left leg. There were probably other fractures of the feet, toes, hands and fingers. The ice had indeed been hard on him.

I cast my eyes up the ridge and saw that Caspar and Raymond were making good progress to where we had left the sled. Unhampered by the slower pace of Hadar and Kali, let alone the dragging of the sled, they had almost reached it.

Hadar appeared to be getting cold, as his colour was blanching and his lips and nose were turning blue. I took off my own coat and placed it over him. He was still unconscious, breathing steadily, although shallowly, and according to Kali, his heart was maintaining a rapid but regular beat.

Raymond and Caspar had reached the sled and seated themselves upon it with their legs out to the sides. They launched themselves down the slope, and then used their feet to brake and steer the sled in our direction. Their descent was quite spectacular to watch, and twice almost ended in an upturned disaster. Raymond was yahooing with the thrill of it. It did not take them long to bring the sled down the slope and brake it a few yards from where we were.

With the exception of our few medical supplies, we unloaded everything from the sled. We would carry most of it ourselves. Slowly, and with infinite care, we were able to manoeuvre Hadar's unconscious form onto the sled.

'Now what do we do? Do we go back down to Kali's village?' asked a troubled and upset-looking Ruth.

'Ahem,' said a new voice behind us.

13

We turned as one to see a short man with a shaved head. He was dressed in a heavily patched maroon robe that fell about his left shoulder, leaving his right shoulder and arm uncovered. Around his waist was wrapped a similarly patched cloth that fell to just below his knees. He wore only sandals on his feet. Despite this scanty apparel, he did not appear at all cold.

Kali attempted several words of greeting in the different languages of the region, but none gained any recognition or reaction from our new arrival. Instead, he raised his hands and placed them palm to palm, bowing his head as he did so. With a gesture, he beckoned us to follow him. Raymond and I took the reins of Hadar's sled, and along with the others, we followed this unexpected saviour.

The monk, or holy man – for that is what I assumed him to be – led us through a maze of snowdrifts and ice boulders, before we arrived at a frozen cliff face, in the midst of which was the entrance to a tunnel. Our guide did not pause and entered the tunnel, beckoning us on again and smiling as if to say 'Do not be afraid'.

The ice tunnel stretched only about sixty to seventy yards before it came to a stony encasement and continued on through the rock. At various places, torches burned in sconces set into the walls, casting a flickering glow along the corridor. As we progressed, I noticed several recessed rooms off to the side, which were clearly storerooms and had been carved into the mountain. In two of these storerooms, similarly attired monks went about their activities; one of them was working a loom, a craft normally preserved for women in most other cultures.

It was then I realised that I was no longer cold and that I was working up a sweat hauling Hadar on the sled. I observed some beads of sweat on Raymond's brow.

'I didn't think it could be this warm down here. Time to doff these heavy coats,' I said to Raymond, and he called out for a brief halt. Our guide seemed to understand and stood smiling while we all removed our quilted coats.

It was at this moment that Whisper tumbled from Ruth's clothing. Our guide's benign smile changed to one of sheer joy and laughter. He clapped his hands, bringing two of his colleagues from the nearby storerooms. Upon seeing a playful Whisper scampering around our feet, they too both smiled broadly and made gestures to indicate their approval of her presence.

We continued along the underground thoroughfare, taking various turns into other tunnels as we went. I was surprised that despite our depth in the earth, the air around us felt fresh and clean, and cool, but definitely not the cold of the mountainside. There also seemed to be a faint glimmer of natural light filtering in.

We turned into yet another tunnel and, after a short distance, emerged into a large chamber. This, too, appeared to have been carved out of the rock. Looking up to the ceiling, I could see several apertures that opened to the outside of the mountain – presumably, we had passed through to the other side of the slope we had been attempting to climb earlier.

The cavern was well-lit and lined with wooden panels and shelves, upon which lay rolls of bandages, numerous different types of instruments, and jars of varied ingredients, as told by their different colours and textures. A dozen cots, three of which were occupied, confirmed to me that our guide had brought us straight to the monastery's infirmary. He indicated that we should get Hadar up onto a bench that was higher than the cots and positioned directly under one of the light-admitting apertures in the cavern ceiling.

Very carefully, Kali, Raymond, Ruth and I raised Hadar's inert form from the sled and gently laid him upon the bench. Using gestures, our guide signalled that we should remove Hadar's clothing. Once it was clear we had understood this last directive, he turned and left the room. Raymond took his falchion and began slitting the sides of Hadar's leggings. Ruth produced two of her sharp little throwing knives, and we set about carefully cutting and removing his clothing. By some unspoken agreement, we all chose to leave Hadar's loincloth in place.

Our guide returned with an older monk, similarly attired, who placed his palms together and bowed in greeting to us and then, speaking in a northern Hind dialect, said, 'Greetings, and welcome to the Buddha's Smile. I am Kan Do, Master Physician to the monastery. I am told your companion has been seriously injured in a fall. I believe he may require some urgent treatment if we are to help save him.'

'Yes,' I responded. 'Can you help him?'

Master Kan Do moved over to where Hadar lay and commenced his own head-to-toe examination, calling out instructions to his colleague in another language that was unknown to us. His colleague, or assistant, began to gather instruments and a couple of jars from the shelves. The instruments he placed in a pan, which he filled with what smelled like spirits of wine; the jars were placed on a tray next to the cot.

After examining Hadar, Master Do turned to us and said, 'The injury to the side of the head, and its accompanying swelling and purple colour, is a matter of grave concern and urgency. There is quite probably a build-up of pressure from bleeding inside the skull, which can damage the brain within. He must be treated as quickly as possible. Do you wish for me to treat him?'

Neither Ruth nor I had any knowledge concerning the treatment of head wounds such as the one Hadar had sustained. Naturally, we gave our consent for Master Do to do what he could.

Ruth and I stood back with the others while the older man and his assistant began their work. I could tell Ruth was as intensely interested as I in what we were about to witness. Master Do must have noticed our interest and beckoned us closer.

The two monks began by washing their hands and forearms in the spirits of wine before taking a razor and shaving almost the entire left side of Hadar's head, being particularly careful around the growing dark purple swelling. With his hair removed, the disturbing swelling and colour of the traumatised area were even more apparent. Master Do's assistant opened a jar, from which the older man removed a scoop of unguent and applied it to the shaven area, gently rubbing it in. He then took a scalpel and made a two-inch-long incision in the scalp below the swelling, from which fell a large, dark clot of blood that landed with a squelchy plop upon the floor.

Whisper pounced upon the clot, and in a moment, it had disappeared down her throat. Master Do noticed this and said something to his assistant, which made them both briefly laugh. Ruth looked a little horrified at what Whisper had just done.

Master Do then made two other incisions perpendicular to the first and peeled the flap of scalp back, revealing the bony white-pink of Hadar's skull. There was a sudden thump as Kali fainted against one of the nearby cots. Master Do continued his work unabated; Caspar and Raymond picked Kali up and placed him on the cot.

Master Do's assistant handed him a small awl-burr-like instrument. He began to twirl it between his fingers, slowly drilling a small hole in the side of Hadar's head. After only a few short minutes, a fine jet of bright red blood, clearly under pressure, streaked several feet across the room. Master Do waited until the flow of blood was only a small trickle before placing a small drainage wick just inside the hole. Next, he placed a linen pad his assistant had impregnated with unguent over the hole and proceeded to bandage Hadar's head. Whisper was busy cleaning the floor. A gentle moan from the direction of the cots indicated Kali was coming around from his swoon.

Master Do moved down Hadar's body to where Ruth had detected the hardening and swelling beneath the left side of the rib cage. He carefully palpated the area, seeming to take special notice of the boundaries of the swelling. At his request, his assistant held out the jar of unguent, which he applied to the area. He then took a narrow metal tube with a very pointed end from his assistant and wasted no time in plunging it into the swelling on Hadar's side, with another resultant issue of blood and some other fluids streaking away. Whisper was even quicker in cleaning it up.

Master Do did not remove the tube but left it in place to drain into yet more unguent-impregnated gauze. He placed another bandage loosely on top of it.

The light from outside was beginning to fade.

'It is best that your friend is left to rest overnight,' advised Master Do. 'Tomorrow, I will examine and treat his other injuries. Please make yourselves at home here in the infirmary. There are plenty of cots for sleeping, and I will have food and drink sent in for you. My assistant Chandra will be in the next room, should you need anything or have concerns about your friend during the night. It is propitious that you have a messenger of the gods to look over your friend.'

With that, he reached down and gently stroked Whisper's back, smiling broadly as he did so.

14

The five of us took it in turns to watch over Hadar through the night, which was peaceful and uneventful. He did not move in any way nor make any sound beyond the shallow in-and-out drafts of his breathing. The sun was barely up, with only a low level of light making its way into the infirmary, when Master Do and his assistant arrived with another monk in tow.

'Greetings,' said the new monk, bringing his palms together and inclining his head. We reciprocated as one. He introduced himself as Darma and explained that he was to be our primary host and translator when needed.

'Master Darma,' said Ruth, 'we are in need of relieving ourselves rather urgently.'

'Forgive me,' replied Darma. 'Follow me.'

We followed Darma through yet more tunnels, until we reached a curtained outdoor platform on the mountainside, high above the valley. There was a series of holes and handrails set along the platform. Their purpose was rather obvious, and we all allowed Ruth the first use of the 'sky latrine' before the four males in our party collectively emptied bowels and bladders onto the valley floor far below. Buckets of freezing cold water and dried moss were available for our hygiene. It was an unusual experience.

'I have to admit, that smelled much better than any Crusaders' stinking toilet trench I ever had to use,' commented Raymond.

Upon our return to the infirmary, Master Kan Do explained that he was keen to set Hadar's broken bones as soon as possible – those that he could. As Hadar was still unconscious, it was a relatively simple matter of extending each of his limbs past the broken point and realigning the two ends of bone, as best that Master Kan Do's sense of touch could approximate them. Each limb was then bound to a board to hold it straight and in place. Ruth and I carefully noted every stage, while Hadar remained asleep and impassive throughout the setting of all his fractures. Those that we knew of, at any rate.

Master Kan Do spoke briefly with Darma, who turned to us and said, 'Master Kan Do will watch over your friend and asks that I give you a tour of our complex and explain some of our rules and customs. Our Grand Master, the Lama of the monastery, has also requested to meet with you. He asks that you please bring your little companion along with you. I do not see her.'

As if knowing she was being discussed, Whisper wriggled her way up Ruth's tunic and poked her head out, much to everyone's laughter. Ruth placed her on the floor at our feet to follow.

Darma led us along several corridors, all lit by cleverly placed apertures to the sky above us. He guided us to a very long outdoor balcony that was anchored to the rock face of the mountain by huge, thick lengths of timber. The platform was sheltered from the elements by a veranda overhang and was predominantly painted in red on the outside, with greens, oranges and white on the inside. Small coloured flags with an unknown script written upon them flew from the overhang. We had astonishing views to the north, south and west, the east being obscured by the mountain.

'This is the face of the monastery that the outside world sees,' explained Darma. 'When observed from afar, the red rail and balustrade resemble a mouth on the face of the mountain. This is how the monastery came to be known to the people of the valleys below as the Buddha's Smile. It is what we came to call our home as well. To many in the outside world, this red mouth is thought to be the entrance to Buddha's Smile. As you can see, it is inaccessible from below. You have already passed through the real, hidden entrance.'

I realised he meant the maze of snow mounds and the ice cave.

From the balcony, Darma took us down further corridors to a great hall, where dozens of monks were seated with their legs crossed in neat rows. They were uttering some mantra rich in vowel sounds and deep in resonance, which vibrated its way into my body in a manner that was pleasantly pacifying. I could not help but notice that many of the monks' eyes drifted to where Whisper was trying to climb up Ruth's leg and that they all wore smiles upon their faces. The mantra lost some of its metre and magic as a consequence of their distraction.

'The monks who live here are from many different places, speak many languages and dialects and, as you will notice, have differing facial features and skin tones,' said Darma. 'Many of them have sought us out, yet others have found their way here by accident or chance like yourselves and have chosen to stay.'

From the prayer room, we progressed through what appeared to be a large dining hall with rows of cushions and low tables. No one was present. Darma informed us that the monks ate only one meal of rice a day, usually after noon. Being a still-growing teenager, I was not sure how I felt about this dietary regime.

After we exited the dining hall, we followed the growing sounds of human exertion and physical contest. Darma led us into what I can only describe as a gymnasium of sorts. The monks present were engaged in a variety of martial activities, including an incredibly acrobatic form of wrestling where the contestants leapt and flew around each other. Others were engaged in duels with staves and were trying to knock each other over or, it seemed by their efforts, out. In another corner of the hall, monks were engaged in shattering blocks of wood with their bare hands or feet. Caspar and Raymond stood open-mouthed, in awe at the displays of martial prowess going on before us.

'Unbelievable!' exclaimed Caspar. 'How do they do that?'

Darma offered, 'We are a sect of warrior monks pledged to maintain the balance of good and evil in this world, through both maintained ritual prayer and the deployment of disciplined martial skills where needed. There are other branches of warrior monks in monasteries across the Himalayas. Our distinguished Lama will discuss this with you later when you meet him.'

'I don't think I would like to meet your warrior monks in battle,' said Caspar.

'Nor I,' piped in Raymond.

We continued our tour of the mountain's halls, corridors and specialist artisan spaces. We walked the length of a dormitory with neatly rolled grass matts and head blocks where most of the monks slept. There was a library of scrolls, some made of a textile called *paper,* others of thin copper sheets with inscriptions engraved upon their surface. I examined one or two, but the script was meaningless to me.

'From here,' said Darma, 'I would request that we walk in silence, so please, do not talk amongst yourselves. I will quietly explain things as we go.'

We progressed further into the mountain, down a hallway to a point before two large doors, where Darma halted and removed his sandals. He motioned for us to do the same with our footwear, which we did without noise or complaint.

Slowly, Darma opened the doors, and a warm golden glow diffused its gentle light around us. As the doors swung open, I became aware of a great space filled with lit candles and, even more impressively, a host of golden statues, all exactly the same. They were of a cross-legged, seated man with very large ears and a serene and peaceful countenance.

'Behold,' said Darma in a soft voice, 'the Hall of the Golden Buddhas.'

It seemed to me that there was more gold in this one place than I had seen in all the halls of all the magnates I had ever visited. It was astonishing. It was also, somehow, very relaxing. Whether it was the warm glow of candlelit gold or something metaphysical emanating from the Buddhas, I do not know. I could tell from Ruth's expression that she, too, felt at peace in the hall.

Our gentle reverie was ended when Darma turned and led the way out.

Once we had left the Hall of the Golden Buddhas, it was Caspar who raised the question that had been in all our minds since we had arrived. 'Darma. How is it that the monastery is so warm, sitting so high in the ice and snow?'

Darma smiled. 'It is one of the Lord Buddha's blessings bestowed upon our community. Come. I will show you the grottoes.'

We turned into a new corridor and began to descend an old stone stairwell worn smooth by the passage of many monks over many years.

'This mountain is a massive, honeycombed rock of volcanic origins,' he said, waving his hand in the direction of a large, porous outcrop of rock. 'Most of the passages we have walked along were carved out by lava flows long ago, and the halls, as you have seen, were excavated by monks long since passed from this plane. The monastery is heated by underground springs. The warm air that rises from these springs makes its way through vents in the rock, gently heating them and the air around them. Some areas of the community are not as warm as others, but for the most part, the complex is maintained at a pleasant temperature.'

As we descended the stairwell, the air became increasingly humid, and I was not surprised when we exited into a spacious water-filled grotto that steamed with heat. There was a small group of monks bathing or simply relaxing in the water. To add to the atmosphere of the grotto, it was partially lit both by lanterns and by small pale green and yellow lights around the walls and upon the ceiling. Darma informed us that they were glow-worms.

'We must move along. The master awaits us,' said Darma.

15

We traced our steps back through the monastery, stopping at the infirmary to check on Hadar. He was still unconscious and swathed in bandages from head to ankles. Two new monks were assisting Chandra, attending to Hadar's hygiene and comfort. I noticed a pack of some sort had been placed beside the drainage site on the left side of Hadar's head. I asked about it, and after Darma and Chandra briefly spoke with each other, Darma informed us it was an ice pack to reduce the internal swelling around the brain. There was another ice pack over the wound below Hadar's ribs. It was a new idea to me and made good sense. Ice had been a rare commodity in Outremer and India, but was plentiful here, and could combat inflammation.

'Have you noticed how much opportunity we've had for learning different healing arts around here without anyone actually sitting us down and teaching us?' I said to Ruth, almost in disbelief.

'Yes. I know,' replied Ruth. 'Yesterday's surgical procedures were amazing, although I wish with all my heart it was not Hadar who provided the case study.'

Darma beckoned us to follow him, and he led the way along yet more corridors until we arrived at two large doors, which he opened for us. The room was sparsely furnished, with another view of the west and the valley below. Mats and triangular seating cushions were placed around it. The smell of incense was strong in the air. Against one of the cushions sat an elderly man, who smiled openly and warmly upon our entrance. He immediately beckoned us to sit, except Whisper, who scampered over and rolled onto her back in front of him, looking up expectantly at him. He beamed delightedly, reached down and gently rubbed her belly, to which he received a contented purr and a playful swat, and this gave him a jolly laugh. I liked the look of his laughing eyes.

'Welcome to our humble retreat,' he said, speaking in the same northern Hind dialect as Darma. He placed his palms together and inclined his head. 'I am the Lama of the Buddha's Smile, but please, simply call me Li Po. You will notice my brothers, the monks, call me Master Po, but you are not monks and may call me by my given names.'

'Greetings Li Po,' we said, repeating the gestures of hands and head.

Darma made the introductions, Li Po asking polite questions of us at each turn. His smile broadened across his face and his eyes sparkled in amusement. All the while, he continued playing with or stroking Whisper, much to her delight.

'How is your older companion?' asked Li Po.

'Hadar sleeps, and we hope for a good recovery, although I suspect it will be a long one,' I said, thinking of my own recent convalescence.

'Master Kan Do, our head physician, believes so as well. You are all welcome here for as long as his recovery takes, and longer, if that is your desire.'

'Thank you, Li Po,' came our joint reply.

'But you are welcome here anyway, for you have brought great joy to us. The arrival of your little friend here is of considerable significance to our community.'

The Lama must have noted some puzzlement on our faces at this.

'Forgive me. I forget there is much that you do not know. I shall start at the beginning.'

The Lama paused for a moment and then began his story.

'In the distant mists of time, these mountains, these Himalayas, were known as the Great Stone People and were believed to be the homes of the gods of the people who lived within their shadows. All the animals who lived within their arms were believed to be the companions, sisters or brothers, sons or daughters of the gods. These animals came to be considered sacred and are seen by many in this part of the world as the messengers of the gods. The snow leopard is viewed as one of the most sacred, as it roams the highest in the mountains.

'What is peculiar to the snow leopard is that its spirit is closely linked to those of the shamans, our physicians and spiritual healers. It is said that the snow leopard spirit easily walks between this physical world of ours and the world of the spirits, whispering advice to the shamans, particularly if they are praying for guidance. It is of interest to me that you have chosen to name the cub Whisper without any knowledge of this heritage.

'It also appears as more than just an uncanny coincidence that five travelling healers and helpers, one in particular' – he smiled at Ruth – 'have found themselves the guardians of a young snow leopard. What also seems significant is that, like in our own community here, I believe each of you is also something of a warrior.'

At this observation, Kali pointed to himself and shook his head in embarrassment. 'I am just a humble helper and guide,' he declared.

The Lama leaned forward and rubbed Whisper's belly again, then laughed delightedly at another playful swat of her paw.

'A snow leopard has not been seen in these parts in many years, and our community is placing great import upon the return of one. The monks have been talking about nothing else since your arrival. My spiritual brothers and I believe that the gods are moving to intervene here on the physical plane by sending this little messenger amongst us. It is up to us to glean the nature of what the gods wish to tell us and what they wish us to do.'

Li Po paused for a moment, appearing to gather his thoughts.

'Now, I must speak frankly,' he continued. 'Your friend, Hadar, will be many months recovering from the serious injuries sustained in his fall. Master Kan Do is not confident of a full recovery, either, and Hadar may never be able to leave this place due to permanent disability. I am sorry if my candour is upsetting, but truth is the best path in all matters.'

With that final comment, Li Po bowed his head and sat in silent expectation of a response.

Caspar spoke first. 'Li Po, I have a question to ask which concerns our presence in your domain. In our own faraway land, our king was dying of leprosy, and we were commissioned to travel to Hind, as we had been led to believe that a cure was to be found in this country. Sadly, we have heard that our king is now dead. Even so, my colleagues and I are curious to know if there is a cure for leprosy that you know of in this land or, for that matter, any of the lands around us?'

Li Po looked down at Whisper, slowly shaking his head, and then responded, 'If there is such a cure, I have never heard of it, and I doubt that Master Do has either. I am sorry to disappoint you in this regard.'

At this point, Ruth spoke up. 'Thank you for your honesty, Li Po. Naturally, all of us would choose to stay until Hadar is healed or improved, one way or another. We are grateful for your offer of hospitality. I would, however, ask another favour: that Master Kan Do give opportunity for Ippolito, Caspar, Raymond and me to learn something more of the healing arts, of which he has already shown himself to be a master. Then, we may take these skills into the wider world and apply them where needed. I believe Master Kan Do will be able to teach us much that is unknown in our part of the world.'

'Spoken like a true healer, Ruth,' replied Li Po. 'Of course. I think Master Kan Do will be pleased to have such students at his side. There are other practitioners amongst us from whom you may learn other disciplines related to the art of healing. It may be that, in turn, you have skills and knowledge that you can impart to them. I expect it will be a very satisfactory arrangement for all involved.'

'Er, and,' began a slightly nervous Raymond, 'may we also have some opportunity to develop our martial skills alongside your warrior monks? Their abilities are absolutely awesome. We have never seen anything like it in the west.'

'I, too, should like to learn skills to help defend myself and my friends,' volunteered a bolder-than-usual Kali.

Li Po smiled and nodded. Whisper jumped into his lap to seal the deal.

16

Hadar was to remain in a coma for the best part of a year. During this time, his broken bones knitted perfectly – each of his limbs was the same length as its opposite. Master Do was obviously a competent bone setter as well as a competent surgeon. Every day, once the bones were mended, either Ruth, Caspar, Raymond, Kali or I would move Hadar's limbs through their ranges of motion in order to maintain his flexibility, prevent any contractures and keep blood flowing to his extremities. The drainage wick below his left ribs was removed without complications. We were all satisfied that his heart, chest and breathing were healthy and there was no lasting damage to the lungs and other internal organs. The tiny aperture in his skull closed up, and hairless skin slowly grew back over the area.

Master Kan Do's assistants provided Hadar a regular regime of nutrition and hydration, through the very time-consuming process of introducing a few drops of a concoction Master Kan Do had prepared into Hadar's mouth, then tickling under his chin to promote a swallowing reflex. This kept Hadar alive, but the weight fell off him, and it was only a month or two before he was literally only half the man he had been.

Whisper, on the other hand, continued to grow and grow, and it was not long before she was too big to be able to enjoy the warmth and scent of Ruth's breasts. Ruth and I had begun Whisper's obedience training shortly after our arrival at the Buddha's Smile. We had decided that using a combination of voice commands and hand signals, such as Ruth and I had previously employed, was a good idea, particularly if silence or subterfuge was required.

Whisper was an eager learner, realising that paying attention and attempting what was requested by Ruth or me had its rewards – most often a morsel of food, such as a savoury vegetable-and-rice cake, but also a belly rub, a scratch behind the ears or simply a cuddle. Whisper definitely enjoyed affection. She liked to give it as well, usually in the form of raspy-tongued licks.

While she was still young, we kept her claws shortened and dulled, as she inadvertently scratched members of the community when greeting or playing with them. In a short time, she was responding to various verbal and signed commands. 'Cease' – as in 'what you are doing' – 'drop', 'sit', 'come', and 'wait' were amongst the first she learned. This was mostly to keep her behaviour acceptable within the walls of the monastery, although I don't think any of the monks minded her energy.

'She learns quickly and well,' said Ruth to me one day a month or so after our arrival. 'Do you think she might learn other more complicated tasks?'

'Such as?' I replied.

'Identifying objects and bringing them to us.'

Whisper did not disappoint. Within the month, she would bring whatever we requested, provided she could pick it up and carry it in her mouth. She even began to anticipate commands. The first was ensuring our slippers were by our bedside each morning.

'I wonder if she'll do the same with people?' said Ruth, soon after Whisper had mastered this skill with objects.

We organised a trial with Caspar, Raymond, and Kali. Each stood against a different wall in the room. Ruth or I would say their name and make their sign with our hands, and soon, Whisper was identifying the correct person by approaching them and sitting by their side. Whisper's solution to bringing them to us was to grip their clothes in her mouth and gently pull them in our direction. This was extended, upon their own request, to Master Li Po, Master Kan Do, Darma, Chandra, their assistants and, later, others in the community, as they became known to us and, of course, to Whisper.

It was Caspar who suggested the next stage of Whisper's training. 'While her claws are short, we should teach her some attack and defence commands.'

Ruth was not keen upon the idea at first but acquiesced upon realising that it would be as much for her own safety as for ours.

Kali volunteered to be Whisper's adversary. 'Sharks could not kill me. Her mother could not kill me. I doubt that Whisper will do me much harm.'

Even so, we dressed him in two layers of the heavy quilted coats we had been given in his home village, placing a thick cap with face flaps upon his head and gloves upon his hands.

Over the next few weeks, Whisper came to understand and carry out a variety of defensive and offensive commands. We began with an attack command and then, at Raymond's suggestion, modified that single command to several indicating different parts of the body: the arm, hand, leg, throat and groin. This meant that Whisper was trained not just to kill but also to disable. Master Li Po approved of the latter, as it was in keeping with the training the monks undertook.

Whisper's other martial skills came to her naturally. She was, after all, a born huntress, and was innately able to hide, stalk, attack and kill. Ruth would often take her out into the snow at the rear of the monastery, not just for toileting but to go hunting. As Whisper showed each innate behaviour, Ruth would make a sign to go with it.

Whisper soon was able to add 'hide', 'watch' and 'follow' to her list of commands. She did this as quietly as her name suggested.

For a while, she seemed to delight in springing from some hiding spot to ambush either Ruth, Raymond, Kali or me by wrapping herself around our legs and sometimes tripping us up.

At the same time that Ruth and I were attending to Whisper's training, Caspar, Raymond and Kali and I placed ourselves under the tutelage of the Martial Master, Lin Dari, with Darma acting as our interpreter. Ruth chose to absent herself from these sessions. She had her knives, and now, she had Whisper as well; it was enough, she said.

I will never forget the first day of our lessons, when I stripped down to the loose pantaloons worn for martial training and bared the great ugly scar that ran the length of my body. Upon the requests of those in the hall, I stripped down to my loincloth to show the scar in its entirety. Needless to say, it drew many comments and questions from those around me, and one even asked if I had fought with a dragon. I told the story of my encounter with the great sword on Ganesha's tusk at the battle of Gadaraghatta, and Darma translated it. The tale seemed to earn me some kudos amongst the monks, who, despite being highly trained warriors, had never actually been in any armed conflict. I made sure that Darma mentioned Caspar and Raymond's heroics on the day as well.

A lot of the training was more torturous for me than for Caspar, Raymond or Kali. The different exercises, positions and rituals of movement all served to stretch my scar tissue just as painfully as when Raymond pulled on them during my initial rehabilitation back in Anhilwara Patan. Still, I persevered through the pain and was soon learning how to perform some of the highly acrobatic jumps and leaps across the training hall that the monks seemed to do so effortlessly.

The monks' training was not designed to kill an enemy, but rather to disarm and disable them before they were able to kill you, as it went against the monks' beliefs to intentionally take a life without good reason. I found myself gravitating toward the stave as my weapon of preference. It was not long before I was able to perform all the exercises associated with its deployment in a fight.

Raymond had chosen the stave as well. After some weeks, Master Dari decided that it was time for Raymond and me to face off in a duel. We were given padded bands to wrap around our face, head and hands as our only protection. I noticed that our duelling staves were also lighter than the ones we had been practising with.

Raymond and I faced off. Around us, the monks looked on, eager to see two westerners do battle. We briefly clacked our staves together in salute and jumped back into our blocking positions. Raymond swung first, trying to sweep me off my feet. I saw it coming and jumped high before launching a blow to Raymond's side as I landed back on my feet. We both defensively stepped back again.

'One to you,' said Raymond. 'I think I owe you!'

With that, he darted forward and lunged. His stave took me in the midriff, but I spun away, considerably diminishing its impact. Upon completing my turn, I landed another blow, this time across Raymond's shoulder blades.

'Could have been worse,' he commented.

Our duel was a very slow and clumsy affair compared to the ones the monks held. Their staves whirled and swung in a blur of speed and strength when they were competing, and their body movements were of an acrobatic standard that often left my mouth gaping in awe.

'How do they do that?' asked Raymond, as we sat recovering from our duel. 'I mean, jumping so high while spinning in the air, and then turning to land a blow at the same time.'

'I suspect they've had several more years of training than you or I,' I replied.

I was surprised when Kali approached us from the other side of the hall and said, 'Alright, it is my turn now. Which of you will fight me?'

Raymond, with perhaps a little too much condescension, said he would. Kali surprised him, as he was much quicker on his feet than either of us suspected, and Raymond was the victim of even more blows that day. Kali looked very satisfied with his performance at the completion of their match.

After an hour or two of this rigorous and punishing training, it was always enjoyable to take a soak in the steaming waters of the grotto. There, we got to know many of the other monks, as the environment was always relaxed and friendly, and any bruises, broken skin, or painful welts were quickly forgotten between victim and victor.

It was the evenings I enjoyed the most. Ruth and I would attend Master Do in his study, along with Chandra, and Darma would act as occasional interpreter. Once in a while, Caspar, Kali or Raymond would join us. None of Master Do's medical texts were in any language I could read or understand, but Darma helped translate where he could. Many of the papyri, scrolls and books were abundantly illustrated in beautifully coloured prints of human anatomy, both male and female. These far excelled Hadar's copied illustrations that we had studied back in Jerusalem. Master Do also had a local equivalent of the *liber herbalis,* which was just as richly illustrated as Hadar's. Ruth and I surprised Master Do when we were able to explain the properties, preparation and uses of a number of plants that were common to both texts.

Master Do also introduced Ruth, Raymond and me to a form of medical treatment none of us had ever seen or heard of before. It involved the placement of very fine needles at points along what were termed meridians of energy within the body. To demonstrate the effectiveness of this treatment in alleviating pain, he placed two of these needles in his arm and wrist. He then invited Raymond to pass a sharply pointed surgical probe through his hand.

Master Do held his hand up, palm out. I realised he did not want to sever any tendons or blood vessels; the probe would slide by these structures rather than slice them as a knife would. To our amazement, Raymond pushed the probe through the skin of the palm, through the flesh of the hand and out the other side, and Master Do smiled the whole time without even a flicker of discomfort appearing on his face. He signed for Raymond to withdraw the probe, which he dutifully did. There was only the tiniest drop of blood on either side of the hand.

The ramifications of this treatment for everything from the extraction of teeth to the amputation of limbs were immediately apparent to Ruth and me. For a moment, I could not wait to tell Hadar about it, before realising I may never get the chance to. Master Do observed our keen interest in his needles and presented us with our own set, along with some charts that illustrated the numerous points of insertion and the grids upon which the meridians of the body ran.

Over the next few months, Master Do made the needles a point of focus in our learning. Before long, we were becoming competent in treating not just pain, but other common conditions, such as constipation, menstrual disorders, migraines, nausea and vomiting, amongst many others.

It was Ruth who asked the question that had been on both our minds. 'Master Do, is it possible to use the needles to awaken Hadar?'

Master Do's face showed the answer. 'If I could insert the needles into his brain and knew exactly where to place them, perhaps, but I cannot.'

There was nothing we could do for Hadar.

17

Perhaps one of the most significant episodes of learning Master Kan Do offered Ruth and me was the opportunity to explore a human body. Up until this time, we had been exposed only to illustrations, such as the ones Hadar and, more recently, Kan Do had shown us. Ruth and I had seen glimpses of human anatomy on the battlefield of Gadaraghatta and in the aftermath of Godfrey's duel with Gurk, but in each case, the anatomy was not intact.

One afternoon nearly a year into our stay, Ruth and I were in the infirmary, practising with the needles on each other. Whisper was resting at the foot of Hadar's sleeping form, as she often did. There were no ill monks in the cots, and we had the place to ourselves when Master Kan Do and Chandra quietly entered the room.

'Greetings, young healers,' said Master Do warmly, bringing his palms together, to which Ruth and I likewise reciprocated. 'An opportunity has arisen to further your education.'

Ruth and I naturally gave him our full attention.

'Early this morning, one of our monks, Shen Wee, passed from this world in his sleep. It was an unexpected departure, but one that nonetheless presents me with an opportunity to show you and Chandra much about the human body.'

Ruth and I looked at each other, both realising where this was going at the same time. This would probably be a once-in-a-lifetime opportunity, as religious proscriptions in the west forbade the dissection or desecration of the human body, dead or alive. Anatomy dissections and tutorials were done on pigs in the western schools of medicine.

'I can see by your faces that you are already ahead of me. I take it that you have no objection to observing a dissection of Shen Wee's mortal remains.'

'None at all,' I eagerly replied, as Ruth nodded alongside me.

'Very well. Put your needles away and come with me,' he said. 'Your room is on our way. You will need to gather your quilted coats to keep warm, as the body is being kept in a coldroom.'

Master Do led us to a part of the monastery I had not seen before. It was not as well-lit as the rest of the monastery, and it was colder. We soon arrived at what looked like a storeroom door.

On a table in the centre of the room, surrounded by a dozen or more candles, lay the pale body of Shen Wee. I thought he looked very peaceful. Three large bronze pots lay beside the table, and a tray of instruments had been set up beside it. Master Do had anticipated our interest and prepared everything in advance.

Moving up to the table and tray, Master Do beckoned the three of us to move in closer around the body. He had to speak alternatively in two languages for the benefit of Chandra, Ruth and me, and he did so graciously and easily.

'First, let us look at the limbs,' he said, taking a small scalpel and deftly running the blade down the entire length of Shen Wee's leg and foot, revealing a thin layer of yellowy fat lying over striations of pink and red muscle fibres. He made some more judicious cuts, and then, grasping the loose skin around the top of the thighs with two pairs of tongs, he stripped the skin from the leg in two deft tugs. He carefully placed the flayed skin in one of the bronze pots.

'These joints and muscles you see are like ropes and pulleys that manoeuvre our limbs around,' he explained, as he cut into the knee joint to expose the smooth, sliding cartilage that covered the ends of the leg bones. 'If I pull, or shorten, this frontal thigh muscle, the lower leg moves forward.' He demonstrated the action. 'It is the same with all the limbs – ropes, pulleys, levers and pivots. And these limbs are beginning to get very stiff.'

'We call it *rigor mortis* – the stiffening of the body after death,' offered Ruth.

'Thank you,' said Master Do. 'That is about all I will be able to show you of the action of the limbs. Now we will turn to the body proper.'

He moved, scalpel in hand, to the top of the body. As before, he ran his scalpel the length of Shen Wee's torso, exposing the yellow fat and the chest and abdominal muscles below. He then incised the muscles to open up the abdominal cavity. I had seen human bowels before on the battlefield of Gadaraghatta and was unsurprised by the glistening, ropey, purple maze that was presented. Ruth had seen them too. Chandra looked a little bit pale but took some deep breaths and remained standing and observant.

Master Do pointed out the various structures of the gastrointestinal system from the stomach to the anus, indicating in turn the liver, gall bladder, spleen, and pancreas, as well as their various ducts and blood supplies. As he did so, he described their supposed functions within his model of medicine. Once he was satisfied that we had seen enough of these organs, he removed them in a business-like manner with a few simple slices of his scalpel, lifted the glistening masses from the cavity and gently placed them in the bronze pots.

'Now, having done away with the most noxious part of the body, let us turn to the next most noxious,' stated Master Do with some degree of satisfaction.

Shen Wee's body had collapsed in on itself somewhat after the removal of so much body tissue, but within the cavity, we could see two fat, encrusted organs with vessels running from them to what we all knew was the urinary bladder.

'See these two big blood vessels running from the great vessel of the body? They carry blood to these two organs, which are the kidneys. They somehow clean the blood and take the liquid waste down these vessels to the bladder, where the fluid is stored for release as needed.'

I will not go into any more details of the dissection. It was a fascinating and informative session, given Master Do's knowledge of the human body. We were so engrossed we did not notice that several hours had passed very quickly. What did seem unusual was that once all the body parts, including the brain, had been removed and placed in the bronze pots, Master Do proceeded to cut the almost skeletal remains of Shen Wee's body up into pieces that would fit into the pots as well.

'Are these to be burial urns?' I asked.

'No,' replied Master Do. 'They are to carry Shen Wee to his Sky Burial. You may learn of this tomorrow, if you wish to join us in honouring Shen Wee's spirit.'

18

Early the next morning, as I was attending to Hadar's movement therapy and massaging his limbs, I told his unconscious form about the events of the day before and all I had seen and learned. In truth, I was hoping that my observations and the other details of the dissection would somehow penetrate through to his unconscious healer's mind and stir him, but his body remained inert, much to my disappointment.

I'd finished Hadar's massage and reached down to stroke Whisper's ears when Ruth, Raymond and Darma entered the infirmary.

'The monks are gathering for Shen Wee's burial. Are you ready?' asked Ruth.

'Yes. Of course,' I replied.

'Li Po has asked Darma to explain things to us if needed,' added Ruth.

The four of us left the infirmary and made our way to the Hall of the Golden Buddhas with Whisper trailing quietly behind us. Kali remained in the infirmary to keep a watchful eye on Hadar. The doors of the great hall were open when we arrived, enabling us to discretely slip inside and take a seat on the floor at the rear of the hall, from where we could watch the proceedings and, of course, show our respect and gratitude to Shen Wee.

Li Po was leading what seemed to be a prayer in a language that was unfamiliar to Ruth, Raymond and me. Shen Wee's remains were still in their bronze pots and rested in a row behind Li Po. Every so often, Li Po would pause in his prayers and a group of monks seated to his right would begin twirling metal cylinders that gave off a tinkling, ringing sound. Then, as one, they would cease twirling, and Li Po would continue his part of the ritual.

After several repetitions of prayers and tinkling, Li Po sat down. Then began the strangest form of singing, if you can call it that, I have ever heard. The monks were making noises deep in their throats that they somehow modulated, either by moving their tongues, constricting their breathing passages or changing the shape of their mouths.

At first, it sounded like a repetitious and very deep 'Oy Yoy Yoy'. It was an unearthly noise. After listening for a while, I noticed that different sections of the gathered monks were voicing a variety of tones. The overall effect was something like listening to a vocal orchestration. I was reminded of some visiting Byzantine monks who I'd seen chanting in Acre's cathedral in my childhood.

Throughout the singing, Whisper was sitting upright with her eyes closed. She had an almost beatific look upon her face, as if to suggest the music was the most heavenly sound on Earth.

This vocal orchestration went on for a while, but it stopped suddenly, to be replaced by total silence. At a signal from Li Po, six monks arose and approached the row of bronze pots, bowing slowly and respectfully to them. As one, each monk grabbed the handles of a pot and lifted it in a single fluid movement.

Li Po led the cortege from the hall. Raymond, Ruth, Darma, Whisper and I moved aside respectfully as they passed through the door, and then we silently trailed behind.

The party moved through the halls and corridors till we exited from the ice cave entrance. From there, we made our way up a nearby peak. It was a slow walk of over an hour. Every so often, one of the monks would blow a long, mournful note on an ornate and somewhat oversized brass horn, as if announcing to the sky and heavens that the dead were on their way.

As we neared the summit, Li Po called a halt, and Shen Wee's remains were gently poured out of their pots, onto the snow. I did not notice Whisper at first, but she had moved through the ranks of monks and approached the remains. The monks stood in an expectant silence as Whisper put her head down and began to lick up the red, bloody fluids that had leaked from Shen Wee's flesh. There was a collective intake of breath and some quiet but joyful 'ohs' and 'ahs' from the monks. Whisper's intervention was, apparently, seen as a sign of fortunate portent for Shen Wee's spirit. More prayers were said, punctuated with twirling, tinkling and deep-throated vocalisations, before the party turned around and headed back down the slope to the monastery.

Needless to say, we were all hungry and tired after climbing to the summit and back that day. I thought of how much more exhausted the pot-bearers would have been. The three of us went straight back to the infirmary to check on Hadar. We were in the middle of relating all we had seen, heard and participated in to Caspar and Kali when Darma rejoined us.

'Master Po sends his blessings and thanks for your respectful presence today,' said Darma. 'He would have come himself, but he is undertaking silent prayer for Shen Wee's spirit for the next two days. He and the other monks are confident our brother's soul will be reborn to a better life, thanks to the participation and presence of Whisper as a messenger of the gods.'

Darma smiled at us. 'Master Po also asks that I answer any questions you may have about our funeral customs.'

'What will happen to the body of your brother on the mountain?' asked Ruth straight away. 'We were expecting some kind of burial or cremation, as happens in our own culture.'

It was the question the three of us had on our minds.

'What you witnessed today we call the Sky Burial, where the deceased is left in a very high place so to be closer to the gods and to heaven. For us, death is the most important event in our lives. We believe the manner of a person's death and the rituals conducted at their funeral ceremony are important in obtaining a more fortunate rebirth, thus enabling their soul to continue making progress toward enlightenment, which is the goal of our belief system.

'In death, the body is selflessly given to the world. We expose it, so it may be eaten by the less fortunate souls of scavengers, such as vultures, eagles, crows, wolves, and bears.

'I and my brother monks have been saddened by the loss of Shen Wee, but we have taken joy away with us today, knowing that our prayers and rituals have been seen and heard by a messenger of the gods. We are happy that our brother will in fact return to a more fortunate life, thanks to Whisper taking in some of his essence.'

'I would like to hear more about this,' said Caspar. 'For a long time, I have felt my own beliefs and those of my church have seemed somewhat hollow and inadequate, even hypocritical.'

'I would be happy to share my beliefs with you,' replied Darma.

Caspar's statement made me think of Rudolphus and everything he had revealed to me about the Latin Church in Rome. Our conversations and his revelations now seemed like a lifetime ago.

19

Ruth and I said our goodnights to Caspar, Kali, Darma and the still unresponsive form of Hadar. My legs were absolutely aching after going back and forth up the mountain, and I was sure Ruth's were as well. I thought she was a little pale, which I took to be caused by fatigue, and she was rather quiet. We both collapsed into bed, too worn out to make love, beyond a sweet little kiss as our heads hit the pillows.

My dreams were disturbed. Darma's account of scavenging animals devouring the bodies of the dead monks on the mountain must have lodged itself in my mind, along with a delayed reaction to the blood and body parts of the previous day's dissection of Shen Wee. In my dream – I should say my nightmare – my friends and I were all dead. Except we were not. Our eyes were wide open and looking around. The monks were intoning their 'Oy Yoy Yoy' chant over our bodies. They reverently picked us up, as they had their deceased brother, and placed us on their shoulders to carry us up the mountain. They laid us in the snow and began their prayers over us. Then they left.

Various scavenging birds and animals came by: vultures, crows, bears, wolves and wild dogs. They stood over, on, or around us, individually or as a group. It seemed each one inspected us and decided we were not worth devouring before moving away. From behind them appeared a much larger-than-life and more ferocious-looking Whisper. She moved around our little graveyard, sniffing us and the air. She then seemed to choose my body from the others and, padding her way over, commenced to lick the blood from my wounds before giving me a strong nip across my fingers.

I woke up with the shock of it. I looked at my hand. By the candlelight, I could see blood on my fingers and Whisper by my bedside. I was a bit confused and angry with her at first, but then I realised there was a sticky, gooey sensation around my thighs and buttocks. I put my hand by my side and brought it back out to see it smeared in blood.

I immediately whipped the covers off the bed, and by the dim light of the bedside candle, I could see that Ruth was bleeding heavily from her vulval region. She was deathly pale and non-responsive to my entreaties to wake up. The bottom half of the sheets and bedding was soaked in blood.

'Whisper! Master Kan Do. Here,' I snapped at her, and immediately, she bolted from our room, without me signing the message as well.

The first thing I did was remove the clothes from Ruth's lower body. I then gathered up the sheet, rolled it tightly into a rather phallic-looking arrangement and introduced it into her vagina in an attempt to stem the flow of blood.

Ruth had grown even paler, and her breathing had become shallow and rapid. She occasionally mumbled incoherently and moaned as if in pain and did not respond to anything I asked of her. She was slipping away from me.

As I was raising the foot of the bed to encourage the flow of blood to her head and vital organs, and away from the bright, incarnadine deluge between her legs, Master Kan Do entered the room. I barely noticed him before he quickly took the scene in before him, said, 'Press down hard on her lower belly,' turned and ran back out.

While I pressed hard on my beloved's belly, Whisper moved to the head of the bed and began vigorously licking Ruth's cheeks. It seemed to rouse her a little, as she moved her face away from the raspy tongue.

Time seemed to drag, and dreadful fears ran through my mind.

After what felt like ages, Master Do and Darma hurriedly entered the room. Master Do carried a bag of some sort, to which was attached a hose-like arrangement with a nozzle at its end. Darma carefully carried a bowl of liquid. The fluid was a pale, greenish yellow in colour. As instructed by Master Do, Darma poured some of it into the bag Master Do was holding.

Master Do spoke quickly. 'Remove the padding cloth from her.'

I did as he requested and took the bloody sheet from between Ruth's thighs, releasing another flow of her precious life fluids.

'Please open her legs,' ordered Master Do, holding the hose by the nozzle.

Darma and I took a knee each and spread Ruth's legs. Master Do immediately introduced the nozzle into her vagina with one hand and with the other squeezed the contents of the bag. This produced a jet of fluid that flowed into Ruth and back out again. Master Do repeated this process several times, until the bloody red back-flow from Ruth's vagina lightened to a dark pink and then to a very pale pink. Master Do removed the nozzle and inspected Ruth's vulva. The blood flow had ceased. Ruth was unconscious but breathing steadily. I felt the pulse in her neck, which was rapid and fluttering, and she was still deathly pale.

Master Do looked at the blood on me, all over the bed, and still dripping onto the floor before saying, 'She has lost a lot of blood, but with rest, I believe she will recover.'

I sent a prayer of thanks from my heart and my head for her delivery. I knew it had been a very, very close thing.

'Master Do,' I tentatively asked, 'what has happened to Ruth?'

'From what looks like a large clot there on the sheet, I believe she has had a miscarriage.'

I was speechless.

Gathering myself together, I asked, 'W... W... What?' indicating the fluid in the bowl.

'Herbs that make the flesh contract. This causes the muscles to tighten around the blood vessels and thus helps stem the flow of blood.'

A herbal astringent, I thought. It could treat many wounds. I would have to ascertain the ingredients and preparation later. I thanked Master Do and Darma profusely for saving Ruth's life before they left the room for the night.

Ruth slept on, and after replacing the bedclothes and giving her as thorough a bed-bath as I could without overly disturbing her, I spent the rest of the night keeping vigil by her side. Whisper lay down by my feet and stayed awake with me. I was glad of her company.

20

Ruth slept well into the next morning. I had not left her side for one moment. Master Do, Darma and Raymond had all been to visit but had left after being assured that she was recovering and that there had been no further bleeding.

Ruth's eyes opened slowly, blinking several times before focusing on me. I smiled as best I could despite my fatigue and concern and gently squeezed her hand. She returned a feeble smile.

'Thirsty,' came her parched voice.

After all the fluids she had lost the night before, I was not surprised she was thirsty, and I poured a small tumbler of water from the pitcher beside the bed. I helped her sit up against some pillows and drink.

'Slowly, Ruth. Slowly,' I said. 'Just sips, or you may vomit. Your body needs to recover.'

She took it slowly, and each swallow seemed to revitalise her a little bit. Finally, she was able to ask, 'What happened?'

I hesitated, confused by the revelation of her pregnancy and not wanting to distress her with the details. Finally, I settled on, 'You had a massive vaginal bleed during your sleep last night.' I did not want to mention the word pregnancy.

A pained look came into her eyes. Then she slowly said, 'So, I lost the baby?'

I could not help it, and I blurted out, 'I didn't know. Why didn't you tell me?'

I had not wanted it to sound like an accusation or a recrimination, but it did, and I immediately regretted the outburst and my lack of sensitivity.

'I was only sure of the baby growing in me in the last day or two, when my second moon flow did not come. I was going to tell you the night before last, but we were both so exhausted after Shen Wee's dissection it didn't happen, and it was the same last night. After the Sky Burials, I was simply too tired and fell straight to sleep. It must have been all the tramping up and down the slopes. Perhaps it somehow dislodged the baby.'

'It doesn't matter,' I replied. 'I love you so much, and I almost lost you last night. I am just so glad you're alive.' And with that, fatigue, shock and relief bubbled up inside me and tears started to well in my eyes. This had a cascading effect on Ruth, as she began to weep as well.

We lay on the bed, just holding each other, sometimes gently stroking each other's face or hair and sharing the gentlest of kisses. There was no more need for talking. Soon, we had both fallen asleep, despite the fact it was late morning.

It was Darma and Raymond who inadvertently woke us, bringing a bowl of what Raymond called 'Master Do's special broth for Ruth'. He gave me two rice cakes as well.

'Master Do also requests that you take a spoonful of this three times daily before meals,' Darma informed Ruth, holding up a clay vial.

'What is it?' I asked.

'He said it was a tonic to stimulate bone marrow. I'm not sure why, but he said something about blood being made in the bones. He also requested that I inform you he will visit later to treat Ruth with the needles so that he may further stimulate the bone marrow.'

Tactfully, neither made any further reference to Ruth's misfortune from the night before, and they left us to our privacy shortly after.

Later, as promised, Darma returned with Master Do. Ruth and I paid close attention to his ministrations with the needles, asking him questions and learning about the restoration of blood. Neither Ruth nor I were too tired to take this in, as we could both see its value in restoring the badly wounded and those, like Ruth, who had undergone considerable blood loss.

Eventually, the treatment was concluded, and the two of them bade their farewells. Ruth and I simply went back to sleep, wrapped in each other's arms.

Ruth felt well enough to try and get out of bed the next morning. First, I dispensed her morning dose of Master Do's tonic.

'Yuck!' complained Ruth. 'It may be restoring me, but it definitely doesn't taste very nice. Nor does it smell all that good, either.'

'Yes. But you have a little more colour in your face this morning, and your eyes are shining again.'

She was still very pale, but I wanted to reassure her that all would be well.

Ruth wriggled to the side of the bed and placed her feet on the floor. I moved beside her, ready to catch her should she swoon. She slowly got to her feet and stood unassisted.

'See!' she happily exclaimed, which was then then followed with, 'Ooh, whoa,' and she suddenly sat back down on the side of the bed.

'Let's just work on sitting up in a chair for now,' I advised.

I placed one of the few wooden chairs around the monastery next to the bed and assisted her onto it without any further mishap. Just as I placed a blanket across her lower half, Whisper entered the room and jumped straight up onto her lap.

'Oh. You are getting too heavy, my precious,' she said to Whisper.

Whisper sat up, as though offended by any suggestion of being overweight, but then, just as quickly, she turned and licked Ruth's chin before snuggling in against her breasts. Ruth gently stroked the leopard's back and scratched behind her ears. I had not cleaned the room, the bed or Ruth as thoroughly as was possible, and I was surprised Whisper showed no inclination to lick the patches of Ruth's blood, in light of how she had partaken of Shen Wee's and readily gobbled up the clot from Hadar's scalp when it fell to the floor in the infirmary nearly a year ago. Then, I supposed, she had been a lot younger.

Master Do, Raymond and Darma arrived at the door, and I invited them into the room. They were all pleased to see that Ruth was out of bed, and they commented that she was looking better. Whisper leapt off her lap and went to Master Do, rubbing her head against his leg. He reached down and scratched her ears, and she settled by his feet as he sat on the side of the bed. I couldn't help but think she was thanking him for saving Ruth's life.

'So, how are you this morning?' asked Master Do.

'Wobbly! At least if I stand up too soon or too quickly,' replied Ruth.

Do nodded. 'And the bleeding?'

'It has ceased,' replied Ruth with some modesty.

'Any pain or discomfort?'

Ruth shook her head, to which Master Do smiled and nodded – indicating, I hoped, that Ruth was recovering and all would be well.

21

It began as a faint creaking and then a series of cracking sounds, which lasted for a minute or two. Raymond and I were working out with our staves in the exercise hall. We paused our bout, just as a very loud crack rang out, followed by an even louder crashing. What came next was a strong gust of cold air that billowed through the corridors and halls of the Buddha's Smile. I learned later on that the cold gust blew half the candles out in the hall of prayers.

Intuitively, I knew something had happened at the ice cave. Raymond and I left the hall and were joined by a dozen or so others who had drawn the same conclusion as us and were racing toward the ice cave entrance.

It was as we had feared. The roof of the ice cave had collapsed in on itself. The monastery's exit to the outside world was blocked, and we had no idea by how much ice. Was it just a few yards and easily cleared, or had the whole seventy or so yards of tunnel collapsed, effectively trapping us? If so, it could take weeks, or even longer, to dig our way through to the outside.

It was only a moment or so after our arrival that a breathless Li Po arrived, trailed by the other masters, who had obviously all been in some meeting. Li Po said something which I did not understand, as Darma had yet to arrive, but from his tone, I suspect it was something like, 'What do I do with this?'

The ice sat in great chunks ranging from fist-sized to a yard or more in length. Suddenly, we heard the creaking and cracking of ice breaking again from within the frozen cascade. We all immediately stepped back and away, despite being within the security of the rock cave. We heard more sounds of ice groaning and eventually falling coming from even further away.

'I suspect,' said Raymond, 'this may be a complete collapse of the ice tunnel. The sounds coming from within are distant and deep. Caspar worked as a sapper engineer before joining the Knights of St John. He'll know about digging tunnels. We just don't want him collapsing them the way they do to break down a castle wall.'

'Tell Darma. He's just arrived,' I observed.

Raymond spoke with Darma, and Darma spoke to the masters. Shortly after, Darma led a small group of monks to the infirmary and returned with Caspar. Whisper and Ruth, now well recovered six weeks after her miscarriage, must have stayed back to keep an eye on Hadar.

Caspar moved around the ice spill so as to survey it from different angles. He yelled loudly into the tumbled ice and tapped some of the larger blocks with the handle of Raymond's falchion, listening to the quality of the sounds. This, he said, was to gauge the density of the ice fall and the likelihood of any further subsidence within it. He did offer the caveat that he was used to reading the sounds of earth, rock and clay, not ice.

'Darma,' said Caspar, 'I would like to meet with Raymond, Ippolito and the masters to plan the excavation of a new ice tunnel. I gather there is no one else here with any expertise in these things.'

Li Po led us to his studio overlooking the plains and the valley far below. We seated ourselves on his triangular cushions around the low table. The masters had obviously been in a meeting here before the ice fall, as there were some scrolls on the table, along with three tumblers and a jug of water. Li Po indicated Caspar and Darma should sit either side of him and then motioned for Caspar to begin, with Darma translating for all.

'Li Po,' said Caspar, 'what tools do you have here that we could use to dig into the ice?'

Li Po looked thoughtful for a moment then said, 'There is not much. We have some staves, such as we use in training, that have metal billhooks and tips.'

It appeared these were the only metal tools the monastery possessed that would be capable of breaking through ice. Added to that, we had two swords, although none of us were keen to damage a good sword with this kind of work.

'The metal-tipped staves will have to do, although it will be slow work, as the blades aren't very big,' continued Caspar. 'What do you have in the way of buckets or other vessels to carry ice and water away from the excavation site?'

Li Po brightened. 'This is not a problem. The kitchen has numerous cooking pots and bowls, and every monk has his own food bowl.'

'That's good. We have the very basics of the tools we need to do the work, albeit painfully slowly. Some picks and shovels would have been helpful. There is, however, one much bigger problem.'

Low, ominous groans escaped some of the masters around the table.

'The ice is no longer compact and solid,' began Caspar. 'Any attempt to tunnel into it will simply see more ice fall and probably cause further injuries or deaths. There are two things we can try to prevent this, and I think a combination of both will be the safest.

'Before we attempt to break into the fallen ice, we need to consolidate it as much as possible. It will freeze and bind any water lightly hosed or sprayed into it. This way, we can turn many separate blocks of ice into a mass that will be much more solid and safer to work with. Instead of fighting fire with fire, we will be fighting ice with ice. So, any ideas on how this can be achieved?'

This caused some further discussion. Both Master Do and Master Dari came up with solutions. I had seen Master Do's used on Ruth to deliver the herbal astringent; he said he had a number of nozzles that would create either a spray or a stream to project the water. Master Dari pointed out that the kitchen had two large hand bellows that could do the same thing.

'Excellent,' said Caspar. 'The second thing we're going to need is wood. We will need to craft uprights and roof struts as structural support for the tunnel so we can chisel our way out. We cannot rely on the strength of the ice we create alone to hold the roof above our heads. How much good strong timber is there in the monastery that could be used for such a purpose?'

Again, there was consternation as the masters considered this. Darma listened intently and then, speaking alternatively in two languages, listed the sources of suitable wood: the tables and benches from the dining hall; cots, bunks and beds from the dormitories and infirmary; shelving and uprights from the scroll stacks in the library; and tables and furniture from the masters' rooms and other parts of the complex. It was quite a long list by the time Darma came to the end of it.

'This is good. Better than expected,' said Caspar. 'Tomorrow, Master Dari, I want you to organise four details of monks: a small one of five or six to operate the bellows and as many of Master Do's medical contraptions as he has, another to bucket away the excess dirty water, and another to bring fresh cold water. Finally, we'll need another group to start stripping and breaking apart all serviceable timber in the monastery. We'll stockpile it and try to think of ways to shape and secure it in the days to come.'

With that, the meeting was suddenly over.

22

Efforts to rebuild the ice tunnel proceeded like clockwork. The masters organised the monks into various work parties, charged with spraying down the ice, bucketing water in or out, picking and chipping away at the ice or erecting wooden uprights and crossbeams against the tunnel walls and roof. By the end of the first week, the tunnel had progressed more than ten yards. On the whole, it seemed to be structurally sound and holding up well.

During this time, Ruth had some problems with keeping Whisper properly fed, toileted and entertained. The still-growing snow leopard was used to exiting the monastery at her leisure to hunt, toilet and generally let off the steam that a healthy young feline would want to. In the first couple of days, she had pointedly turned her nose up at the offering of rice cakes, which were all we had to feed her. By the third morning, she had got over her squeamishness and ravenously devoured them.

Toileting Whisper was more easily solved, and she determined it herself. She simply visited the terrace balcony. As needed, she would make her way to the edge and pivot so as to point her rear end under the rail. From that position, she would let her spray or scat fly to the valley below. This greatly amused the monks taking their rest in the balcony hall.

It was in the second week that we encountered our first obstacle. It initially appeared as a grey and brown shadow in the ice, and it was large enough to be obscuring three quarters of the planned tunnel's path. Caspar advised caution to the pickers who were chipping away with their bill-hooked staves. Gradually, they revealed the very furry coat of an animal – an extremely large, long-dead animal that was frozen solid in the ice.

As the monks chiselled away at the ice and it fell from the tangle of the creature's fur, it became apparent that we had uncovered the animal's rear end. The back legs were folded beneath its body, revealing a short tail and two heavily padded feet, each with four rounded toenails.

'Caspar. Do these remind you of elephants' feet?' I enquired after we had done a quick examination.

'They certainly do,' he replied, 'but I have never seen an elephant this size, nor one with so much long, thick and shaggy hair. It certainly would have kept it warm up here. Its flesh is frozen solid like a rock, and it will probably have very large bones. We're better off not wasting time trying to work our way through it; instead, we should go around the body. This sort of thing used to happen when we were sapping castle walls. Quite often, we would encounter large boulders under the ground that obstructed our path. We soon learned it was quicker to go around them rather than try to smash or cut through solid material.'

Caspar spoke to Darma, who directed the work team to concentrate their efforts to the right side of the beast and move around it from there.

Later that day, we were called to the ice face again. The monk who had drawn our attention indicated to the body, and there, underneath its fur, could be seen a much smaller footpad.

'Mother and calf,' observed Caspar. 'I'm beginning to get a picture of what may have happened here. It would appear that they were caught in an avalanche, and the mother moved over the calf to protect it before they both became buried and frozen here forever beneath the ice and snow.'

As our chiselling and chipping progressed, we became more and more aware of the immensity of the furry elephant. It was easily twice the size of any we had seen in India, and that included the queen's mount Ganesha. One notable difference we observed when the side of its head was uncovered was that its ears were much smaller than the great flapping appendages on the Indian elephants.

If its ears were small, its tusks were much longer, and curved in an upward direction. They were not the lovely white ivory of a living elephant's but had been discoloured by time to streaky shades of brown, black, blue and yellow. Even so, they still had a soft, satiny sheen, like a tusk of living ivory.

We spent three whole days detouring around the two carcasses before we had our tunnel proceeding along its planned course. Master Dari was for digging the great beasts out of the ice but was persuaded against this by Caspar, who rightly pointed out that all he would achieve would be another collapse of the ice above us.

Whisper's feeding issues were resolved after the discovery of the frozen elephants. The morning after their discovery, the monks returned to the site to find that the mother elephant's tail had clearly definable teeth marks in it and was partially gnawed away despite its frozen state.

'You can't blame her,' defended Ruth, on seeing the evidence.

'No. We can't,' replied Master Dari, who then picked up one of the bill-hooked staves and hacked the rest of the tail off. 'I will give this to the cook and instruct him to boil it separately with the rice for Whisper's cakes. It may make them more palatable for her, and we can always slice more flesh as needed.'

The suggestion worked. Whisper was not all that fussy of an eater.

23

The work on the tunnel continued at a steady pace over the next weeks. The five or six monks at the 'front line', or ice face, maintained a unified and almost rhythmic 'raise, blow, chip and scrape' drill. After every few feet of progress, they would lay down their tools and have a short break while the water-spraying team would move in and direct their nozzles into the cracks and crevices in the fall of ice.

While the sprayed water was quickly cooling and freezing the ice into a compact mass, the structural support team was constantly busy erecting uprights and crossbeams to provide additional safety and support. Another team was busy filling pots with the watery slurry from the excavation and carting it away to be thrown over the Buddha's balcony.

'If only soldiers could work in such a disciplined and conscientious manner,' commented Caspar. 'Castles and fortifications could be built in half the time it takes our forces to do it.'

'And,' added Raymond very cheekily, 'there would be no need for knights and supervisors to stand around doing nothing except yelling at hard-toiling soldiers and squires under a hot sun.'

Caspar took the remark with a smile and a small laugh. It occurred to me that back in either of the armies facing each other in Outremer, such an exchange would not have been possible without punishment being inflicted.

In between training in the martial arts, exercising and massaging Hadar's inert form, and sitting and studying under Master Do, I still found time to join the teams and contribute my own labour to the clearing of the ice tunnel, as did all members of our group, including Ruth, who was fully recovered from her miscarriage by this time. It amused me each time I passed the 'hellofalump' – for that was what Raymond had dubbed the strange furry elephant-like creature in the ice – as its rump was slowly being sliced away to provide food for Whisper.

At long last, the day finally arrived when the monks broke through the ice into the fresh mountain air. We had known we were getting close by the changes in the light and colour of the ice. The moment brought a rousing cheer of approval and joy from all those working at the face and along the tunnel. The first through the break in the ice and out into the snow was an eager Whisper, who bolted away in a long-overdue hunt for some fresh meat and warm blood. She did not come back until much later in the day, when she looked very satisfied with herself, presumably having eaten her fill of either snow hares or pigeons. I doubted, after all this time, that there would have been anything left of Shen Wee to interest her.

The last uprights and crossbeams were put in place, and Caspar did a final inspection, ordering further structural reinforcement where he felt there could be some weaknesses, such as around the 'hellofalump'.

I think everybody who was able made a journey that day just to stand in the weak sunshine of the mountainside, enjoy its gentle warmth on their faces, breathe the fresh, clean air and feel the slight breeze on their skin. There was an almost immediate tangible change in the atmosphere within the monastery. Monks who had quietly and stoically endured being cooped up inside and having to work at the ice face were now all chatting excitedly with each other, clapping their hands with joy, and one or two were even doing little dances of celebration in the snow.

The party atmosphere continued that evening as we all sat on the floor in the dining hall. Li Po had made a special dispensation and had several large pots of a tea the monks referred to as 'Bhang' brewed up and shared around the hall. As I later learned, the Bhang tea was made from the same plant that the assassins we had encountered in Persia made their hashish from, but it was not as potent or as hallucinogenic in effect. Instead, it filled all present with a light-headed feeling of wellbeing and relaxation. Conversation, laughter and a joyful camaraderie of brotherhood and oneness were the order of the evening.

Later that night, Ruth and I further enjoyed that joyful oneness with each other.

24

The ice tunnel held up well in the weeks following its completion, and I think Caspar finally settled into a confidence that it was structurally sound. He had been in the habit of walking the length of it every day, closely inspecting ice and wood for any cracks or other signs of weakness. The now almost-rumpless 'hellofalump' still remained as something of a curiosity, although it had slightly changed in appearance. Those parts of its thick, shaggy fur coat that could be reached by the monks had been shaved away and washed, and now stuffed various cushions and mattresses in the infirmary.

Caspar had taken his long sword to the tusks and, after considerable effort, had cut them away from the head. From the huge lengths of aged ivory, the monks had set about making utensils such as spoons and chopsticks, as well as small ornamental symbols to be worn as charms. Other more gifted artisans within the community had carved small statuettes of the Buddha, which were placed alongside the Golden Buddhas in their hall of worship. I even tried my hand at carving and produced a bracelet that I engraved with two overlapping hearts. Needless to say, it was a gift of my love for Ruth. It pleased her greatly, being the first piece of jewellery, aside from her crocodile-tooth necklace, she had ever owned. She claimed she liked it best because I had made it and given it to her, and the crossed hearts were an emblem of what she knew we felt for each other.

It was while I was carving the hearts on the bracelet one afternoon on the terrace balcony that I noticed a small band of travellers traversing the valley floor below, heading in a westerly direction. I did not think a great deal of it at the time. Over the next few weeks, the frequency of individuals and small groups traversing the valley, always heading west, increased. Some were just on foot, while others hauled small handcarts and sleds. Other groups herded cattle, ponies, goats, sheep and pigs before them. One of the groups was particularly large and was probably the population of a good-sized village, plus livestock. I wondered if this was simply a seasonal migration of peoples, such as the Bedouins maintained in the deserts of Arabia, or whether they were refugees fleeing some crisis in their homelands.

During one of my morning sessions of maintaining the movement in Hadar's limbs, I heard the sound of a gong being struck three times. I had not heard this in the monastery before and wondered what it meant. There was only Hadar and me in the infirmary and, not wishing to leave him alone, I simply continued with his stretches, flexions and extensions.

A short while later, I felt a gentle tug on the bottom of my pantaloons. Ruth had sent Whisper to collect me.

I scratched her ear and made the sign for 'good girl'. After finding Chandra in the infirmary's apothecary, managing to tell him I had to leave, I returned to Hadar and said goodbye to him for the day and left him in Chandra's charge.

Whisper led the way from the infirmary. She took me, rather hastily I thought, to the dining hall, which was obviously serving as the designated meeting place for whatever was happening. Ruth was waiting with Raymond, Caspar and Kali at the back of the hall, and I moved over to stand beside her. Whisper settled herself between our feet.

'What's happening?' I asked my friends.

'I'm not sure,' replied Ruth. 'Darma will be along shortly. He and I were in the library when the gong sounded, and he said he would meet us here.'

I looked around the hall and realised that just about every monk in the monastery must have been there. There was a buzz of excitement, as everyone was no doubt speculating about why the gong summons had been sounded.

Darma joined us just as the buzz suddenly quietened. Li Po and another monk, unknown to any of us and wearing a different type of robe that covered both shoulders, entered the hall and took their places at the main table. They spoke briefly to each other, and then Li Po rang a small handbell and called for everyone's attention. Darma began a quiet translation for us as Li Po addressed the gathering.

Li Po commenced, 'Brother monks, please would you welcome our brother Timogin.'

As one, palms were raised and pressed together as heads went down in peaceful and respectful greeting around the hall. Timogin responded in the same manner, although he appeared fatigued and grave.

He was a short man but very stocky. His arm, shoulder and neck muscles were large and well defined. His skin, particularly his face, was weathered and tan in colour. He maintained that serious look about him that suggested he was the bearer of bad news.

'Brother Timogin has travelled the White Path for many weeks to bring us troubling news from the east,' continued Li Po. 'Our brother has reported to me that there have been hostile disturbances and incursions amongst the Song and Han peoples of the Chin nation. Both these peoples are being threatened by a new force. These hostile newcomers seem intent on destroying the peace that has existed both here and in all the eastern realms for many years.

'Brother Timogin has told me that for the last few years, there have been rumours of conflict between the clans of the steppe.

These are the wild people who live to the far north, both west and east of us. According to these rumours, a new leader has emerged who is intent on uniting all the clans, and he has begun a campaign of conquest into the lands that surround those of his people.

'It appears that this new leader has had unprecedented success in defeating both Han and Song armies, as well as displacing many other peoples, clans and tribes. A large number of refugees are now on the move, migrating eastwards, seeking new homelands. We have all seen the evidence of this migration in the valley below the monastery over the last weeks.

'These now-homeless peoples, despite their own defeat and dispossession, are just as avaricious as those who conquered them. I am reminded of a cascade of the conquered conquering others.

'These landless peoples now present a threat to the peace of our existence here. They are not only seeking grassland to graze their herds of ponies, cattle and goats, but they are also pillaging and plundering whatever human settlements they come upon. There has apparently been great slaughter in the many places they have passed. Most disturbingly, the grand monastery of our Tibetan brotherhood has been destroyed. Many of the monks were slain, and their great golden Buddha has been broken up, smelted and reduced to bars of gold to fill the booty wagons of the refugees' baggage train.'

This news raised a collective gasp of shock and dismay from those gathered in the hall. Ruth gave me a worried look, while Raymond whispered a quiet profanity.

'The particular tribes responsible for the destruction at Tibet are known as the Xi Xia. They are still some weeks away from us. They are travelling slowly, due to their great numbers and, regrettably, the immense weight of their baggage and booty wagons.'

Li Po paused and let the burden of what he had just revealed settle upon the shoulders, and in the minds, of all present in the hall.

He began again, 'I question my leadership in this time. All of us here, myself included, have no experience of conflict on the scale faced by our slain brothers in Tibet. I pray that they may now know the eternal bliss of nirvana.'

With that, the master sat down.

For quite a while, Li Po allowed the monks to debate how to deal with the threat. It was after almost half an hour that Darma stepped forward and indicated he wished to speak to the assembled throng. As he could not address his brother monks and us in two different languages at the same time, we had no idea what he was proposing. It suddenly became clear to us when he turned to indicate our group and clearly said 'Caspar'.

Caspar was initially a little taken aback by the proposal, but quickly composed himself and stepped forward to indicate his willingness to undertake the role.

As Darma told us a little while later, he had recommended Caspar, on the basis of his crusading experience, as a military advisor to Martial Master Lin Dari. Darma's case was quite simple and an obvious conclusion. Caspar was the only person in the hall actually experienced in command in battle and in the logistics of war and defence.

Master Dari nodded to Li Po, who nodded in return, and the hall erupted as all those present thumped their fists upon tables or the floor.

Li Po signed for Caspar to come up to the table where he sat. Darma joined him. With Darma translating for many of the gathered monks, Caspar set out the beginnings of a plan of action.

His first recommendation was to form a war council, which he requested Raymond, Ruth and I be part of. To this were added Li Po, Master Dari, and Master Do, along with the three recognised masters of their particular martial disciplines: Hari Phan, stave master, Chun Ging, bow master, and Wang Li, the master of hand-to-hand combat. Added to this were Darma to facilitate translation and Timogin to provide what further intelligence he could. We were to meet first thing the next morning in Li Po's rooms. With this said, Li Po broke the meeting up.

The next morning, Caspar's first task was to learn as much about the enemy as he could, and he questioned Timogin closely. We were able to learn that the enemy were more akin to a conglomeration of small tribes than a nation of people. Of these Xi Xia, half were horse warriors mounted on small and sturdy steppe ponies, which had a stamina to shame any European pure-bred destrier or palfrey and were able to withstand the icy cold of the mountains. The other half were the women, the elderly, the children, the frail and the sick, who travelled with an oxen-pulled baggage train in extremely large wagons that doubled as living spaces.

Timogin was of the belief that the army had split itself into two forces; one that was taking the White Path of the mountains, and the other, which was skirting the borderlands between the Himalayas and the Takla Makan Desert to the north. The former was an invasive force and the latter a scavenging baggage train.

Caspar continued his interrogation of Timogin onto weaponry and tactics. It seemed the steppe warriors were masters of a particular type of bow made from both bone and wood, which had a very long range, and they were trained from childhood to shoot accurately from galloping horseback. They were also familiar with knife and swordplay, but the bow was their weapon of choice.

Their principal tactic in battle was to send shock wave after shock wave of mounted archers to rain arrows continuously down on enemy forces and encampments. Timogin mentioned their uncanny ability to twist in the saddle and fire arrows over the backs of their ponies, even in retreat. I was reminded of the Parthian shot and remembered that they had come from the east as well.

Caspar decided that what we needed most right now was reconnaissance and determined that Master Dari should send out scouting parties to ascertain the current position and dispositions of the enemy force. It was agreed that the scouts would go out in parties of two or three the next morning to locate and observe the Xi Xia, and then return and report, without making contact and, hopefully, without being seen by the enemy. From these reports, we would begin to make our preparations.

With that, the meeting concluded, so the scouting parties could be organised, equipped and sent out as soon as possible.

<h1 style="text-align:center">25</h1>

After the scouting parties had left the monastery early the next day, Caspar was all business and had Raymond, Ruth, Kali, Darma and me almost run off our feet, along with numerous other monks. His first order of business was to ascertain the monastery's ordnance, stores, and general military strengths and weaknesses.

At the end of the day, our audit was one of mixed blessings. Caspar tabled his report at the meeting of the war council that evening. Darma, as usual, provided the translation.

'Firstly, with the exception of Hadar, every man within the monastery is trained in the ways of a warrior, albeit actually inexperienced in warfare.'

Ruth gently coughed at this statement, allowing Caspar to finish with, 'As is every woman and snow leopard.'

This brought a round of smiles from the faces at the table.

'The problem is that we are a very small group compared to the horde of warriors that we will probably face. All told, we are only one hundred and sixteen. Of that total, all have skills in archery, staves and unarmed combat. This can be broken down to three specialist units consisting of thirty-six archers, forty stave fighters and forty bare-hand fighters. Add to that three swordsmen, one knife-throwing woman and a snow leopard of unknown potential.

We cannot hope to face the Xi Xia in the field and win, so we must look to a defensive campaign and face the fact that we could become besieged. It will depend on the will of the enemy; will they decide on a siege while camped in the cold and snow, or will they be keen to move on in search of warmer and greener pastures? It seems to me the deciding factor will be if they believe there is plenty of booty to be plundered within these walls.'

Caspar placed his hands flat on the table. 'Li Po. Is the Hall of the Golden Buddhas common knowledge outside of the monastery?'

'Not all visitors are shown the hall, as you have been, and visitors are rare,' answered Li Po. 'Despite there being very few outside of here who know of the Hall of the Golden Buddhas, my personal fear is that the invaders, having found the golden Buddha of the Tibetan monastery, will assume that such treasure may be plundered here as well.'

'As I suspected,' said a grim-looking Caspar. 'Which leads to the question – Master Dari, what would you think is the best way to defend the monastery?'

'The enemy would be hampered in the close-quarter fighting that an attack on the Buddha's Smile would entail,' stated Master Dari. 'They will not be able to use their ponies in the snow and around the entrance to the ice tunnel. Because of this, they will lose their specialised archer's advantage of speed, shooting and running. Their much greater numbers of archers will be of little advantage. They will only be able to deploy those that can fit in the width of our corridors, much as we are as well. Their greater numbers would naturally see a slow and bloody attrition of our forces, and I believe they would eventually win through.'

'There is only the one entrance to the monastery,' I said. 'Is it possible to camouflage or bury the entrance so that it cannot be discovered? We could always re-collapse the ice tunnel and dig it out again after the enemy decide to move on. We still have plenty of stores and the terrace balcony to supply air.'

'The idea has merit,' replied Caspar.

There was a short silence before Caspar continued, 'Let us consider this further and discuss any other defensive options tomorrow. Ordnance is my next concern. We have enough staves in store for each man to break three in combat, but getting replacements into the fray presents some problems. Any suggestions?'

There were none. Each face was blank.

'Give it your thoughts till tomorrow, then,' concluded Caspar. 'The good news is that we have enough sacks of rice to feed all of us for a year. Water from melted snow can be easily obtained. Li Po, is it true that in some of the other, cooler grottoes, there may be found blind fish and edible crabs and the like?'

Li Po nodded, despite his disinclination to eat the flesh of any kind of animal.

'Finally – Master Do, how are we stocked with medical supplies?' asked Caspar.

'We have adequate supplies to treat a large number of wounds. Furthermore, the medical staff has recently seen the addition of two very talented young healers and their assistants. It is a shame that their master is still in a coma. I am told he has great skill in healing.'

Li Po looked perplexed for a moment, and then he quietly laughed to himself.

It was as the meeting was about to break up that the door flew open and an animated Kali burst into the room.

'It is Hadar,' he declared. 'He has awoken!'

26

Hadar looked confused and frightened when we entered the infirmary. He clearly did not know where he was, why he was there or who the two bald men in maroon robes standing by his bed could possibly be. Everything would have been strange and alien to him. His eyes were wide, and he was struggling to raise himself up from the bed but barely had the strength to lift the sheet he was lying under. Occasionally, one of the monks would gently place a restraining hand upon him to prevent his tumbling from the bed. My heart almost broke to see this frail and fearful old man trying to make sense of what was happening around him. I knew in that moment how much I had grown to love him by the pain I felt in seeing him in such distress.

Ruth and I went to his bedside, while the others in the room stood back. I placed myself in his line of vision. Initially, there was no sign of recognition from him. Gently, I said, 'Hadar.'

He ceased his struggling with the bed linen and looked intently at me for a long moment. His expression was one of puzzlement, then it slowly changed to the annoyance of someone struggling to remember something important. His lips were making some small movements, but they remained closed, and no words came out.

Ruth took his hand and softly stroked the back of it. Hadar

looked up at her. The puzzled look had returned to his face, when slowly, the trace of a smile began to crease the corner of his mouth.

'Hadar,' I tried again, 'it's Ippolito and Ruth. Your friends.'

The dawning smile upon his face brightened as he cast his eyes back and forth between Ruth and me. It seemed Hadar had recognised us at last.

His lips began again to make small puckering movements, as if they were rusty and stiff from disuse. Then, his mouth barely opening, it seemed he whispered, very slowly, 'Ol… nnn… oof!'

I was uncertain what this meant and was about to speak again when Ruth quietly said to me, 'I think he means you and me – "Ippolito and Ruth" – only he can't get his tongue and mouth to say it properly.'

'Pol an oof,' Hadar said again, and this time, the smile seemed to reach his eyes. Despite our concerns, we smiled and laughed back at him.

He brushed his now-long hair away from his face. He then appeared to consider things for a moment, and I could see his mouth trying to move with purpose before he stuttered, 'O… o… ot pen me?'

It was an obvious question in his situation – 'What happened to me?' – and I understood him straight away.

'Do you remember the fall from the mountain?' I asked him.

Hadar appeared to consider this for a moment before uttering a slow, 'O-o-o… N-N… No.'

Ruth sat by Hadar, stroking either his hand or forehead, while I told him the long story of his fall, of the terrible injuries he sustained, of the monk's finding us and bringing us to the monastery infirmary. His eyes widened when I told him of Master Do's surgery on his skull and stomach and the setting of his broken limbs.

Hadar listened to all of this with an alert interest. At the mention of his broken limbs, he experimentally moved them and wriggled his toes and fingers. I thought he had less intentional movement on his right side, in both the arm and the leg, but I said nothing of it. He, however, gave himself an approving nod, apparently pleased that these parts of him had healed. He then began moving his mouth as the prelude to asking, 'Ow ong?'

'Almost a year,' answered Ruth gently.

'A eah!' retorted Hadar, his face revealing a look of shock and surprise.

The news caused Hadar to become silent for a moment. He then lifted the sheet that was covering him and looked down at what I knew to be a very thin and emaciated body, devoid of any excess fat, with only wasted, ropey muscles.

Hadar was clearly disconcerted by what he saw. I could tell from his face that he was turning things over in his mind, reaching for reasons and solutions. Suddenly, his expression became even more grave, and he turned to me, gently tapped the injured left side of his head and pointed to his mouth. Moisture was welling in the corners of his eyes.

I had no words for him. I wished it was me that was speech affected and lying there in debilitation. I noticed that Ruth was similarly upset, a silent tear running down her cheek.

The silence in the room was broken by Darma, who stepped forward and introduced himself to Hadar and then introduced Master Do. I explained to Hadar that it was Master Do who had performed the life-saving procedures on him. They greeted each other with respectful inclinations of their heads.

Master Do began an explanation and description of what had happened to Hadar, as one physician to another. 'When you arrived in the infirmary, my first priority was the swelling and trauma to the left side of your head. I performed an opening procedure to relieve the pressure inside your skull, but I fear now that the damage was already done. It has been my experience that trauma to the left side of the head can bring about speech and swallowing disturbances of varying severity. I notice that you have some right-sided weakness in your movement, which is also one of the paradoxes of brain injury.'

Hadar nodded, although he did not look very happy.

'Your swallowing has been unaffected by the trauma, but the messages of speech from your brain to your tongue and lips have been disrupted.' Master Do paused for a moment and then continued, 'Are you able to form sentences and words in your head, which simply do not come out of your mouth the way you intended?'

'Hess,' replied Hadar.

Ruth suddenly stepped forward and, placing her hands in front of Hadar's face, made the signs we had used during the time that she was unable to speak. The question was, 'Can you still read my hands?'

Hadar smiled, took a few moments, and then, using his left hand, signed back, 'Yes. I can!'

Ruth, Raymond, Caspar, Kali and I breathed a collective sigh of relief, a smile on all our faces. Darma and the senior monks looked at us in some confusion at this sudden change in mood. I quickly explained that it was a form of communication we had developed amongst ourselves. The monks were suitably impressed with this novel idea and indicated their appreciation and wonder.

Master Do then suggested that we had taxed Hadar enough for the time being and should let him rest. Hadar nodded and made the 'I agree' sign to Ruth and me.

As we were leaving the room, I turned back to wave goodnight to Hadar and noticed Whisper had curled up under his bed and was clearly intent on staying there. I pointed this out to the others, to which Li Po commented, 'The spirit of the snow leopard seeks to dream with Hadar's for a while. Whisper's spirit will help your friend's.'

27

Ruth and I, along with Master Do, made Hadar the centre of our combined attention while the scouts were still away seeking out the Xi Xia. Caspar, Kali and Darma, assisted by a team of monks, were busy organising the monastery's defence. From the outset, Hadar was determined to get back on his feet as fast as possible. His first achievement was feeding himself the next morning, and, as a consequence of consuming a proper meal and fluids, his second achievement was attending to his own toilet and hygiene, at the completion of which he signed, 'I still have my dignity,' and laughed.

He might have had his dignity, but the effort exhausted him, and Ruth and I had to help him get back onto the bed.

'Take a rest for now, Hadar. We'll be back in a while to start your exercises,' I said, leaving the room. I could not help but note that Whisper was no longer under the bed. She had curled herself up around Hadar's feet. I presumed it was to keep his feet warm.

Hadar's initial exercise regime was simple enough. Ruth and I assisted him to rise to his feet, one to each side, until he had the balance and strength to stand unaided. His right side was definitely not as strong as his left, and he tended to fall to that side. I was always there to catch him and hold him up. After a week of standing and balancing exercises, the number of near-falls was much reduced as strength and co-ordination returned to his affected right leg.

Darma had observed our work with Hadar and presented him with two short staves he had cut down to act as aids to walking. Hadar did not progress as quickly, nor as safely, with this aspect of his recovery. Fortunately, one of us was always by his side to help him.

Throughout this time, Ruth and I insisted that as Hadar signed to us, he should also try to make the words with his mouth and tongue. This strategy met with inconsistent results, but nevertheless, there was limited improvement in his speech. It gave us all hope that his speech might someday be restored.

Caspar, Raymond, Kali, Darma and Master Dari were still busy making plans for the defence of the monastery. They reported their progress and their concerns to the war council each evening. It had been almost three weeks since the scouts had gone out, and all had returned as planned to give their reports. The general consensus of those who had seen the army was that they were moving very, very slowly and looked like they would still be two to three weeks away from the Buddha's Smile.

Apparently, the army had left the high White Path that followed the ridgeline of the Himalayan peaks and descended into the snow-covered valleys that ran between them. Safer, but slower, as the snow lay softer and deeper there, making it difficult progress for the Xi Xia's ponies. The scouts reported seeing them stuck in the snow, with their riders having to dig them out or, in some cases, abandon the poor animals to the cold and walk away. Most of the scouts believed that some sickness was sweeping through the army, as their passing showed a trail of vomit, watery faeces and bloodstained mucus. Some scouts had seen troops staggering as if drunk, some even falling from their ponies. The ponies, too, were affected, as their trail revealed similar gastro-intestinal symptoms.

'It would appear,' said Master Do, 'that these men and ponies of the lowland steppes have the sickness that affects those from low altitudes who ascend too quickly. With luck, some of them will die before their bodies become accustomed to the height.'

'Let us hope so,' quipped Raymond.

Caspar's mind was working overtime, and he requested that the scouts draw him a map of the path the army was following, making particular note of the height of ridges and the width of valleys. This was not a particularly successful strategy, as most of the scouts were unfamiliar with the use of pen and paper. Drawing accurate representations of the terrain was simply too much of a challenge. Their diagrams looked like those of children.

It was Master Dari who solved this problem with the suggestion that we retire to the rear of the monastery and have the scouts use snow to mould more accurate representations of the mountains, valleys and slopes. The scouts made up for their shortfalls in drawing by shaping out of the softly packed snow a three-dimensional model of the terrain, which clearly gave Caspar hope for the fate of the Buddha's Smile and its monks.

'I see three clear opportunities to halt the progress of the Xi Xia army,' said Caspar, indicating the places on the model where the valleys narrowed beneath particularly high peaks.

Caspar had clearly recalled the battle of Gadaraghatta and the deliberate landslide the queen, Naiki Devi, had orchestrated to fall upon the army of Mohammed of Ghor and his elephant corp.

'Master Dari,' said Caspar, 'how difficult would it be to set off an avalanche at these points?'

Master Dari's northern Hind dialect was not good, and Darma translated both ways, revealing that Master Dari believed the success of the idea would depend on the ratio of snow and ice lying against the rock of the mountains. Snow was easier to set tumbling than ice. However, none of the scouts, nor anyone else, could give us information to answer this question.

'We need to get back out there,' urged Caspar, 'and determine where, and if, we can set up an avalanche in any of these locations.

Master Dari. Can you organise a fresh team of monks to go out first thing tomorrow?'

Master Dari nodded.

'I need to see these sites for myself,' continued Caspar, 'to determine what we may need in the way of engineering and sapping. Raymond, you will accompany me, and Ippolito, I would appreciate your input in this as well. You seem to see things other people miss. Are you able to let go of Hadar's recovery for a while and join the expedition?'

I knew Hadar was recovering well and Ruth, assisted by Chandra and Master Do, would ensure his continued improvement. I also wanted to play an active part in defending this community that had given my friends and me so much assistance.

I had no hesitation in replying, 'Yes. Of course. Hadar will understand it is vital.'

Raymond smiled and gave me a thumbs up, pleased we would be working together as a team again.

Ruth, however, was not so understanding of this as we lay in bed that night and discussed the upcoming mission.

'There is a whole army of steppe nomads out there who would slit your throat as soon as look at you,' she said emphatically, 'and you want to go out in a small group that would be easily overwhelmed at the first encounter, and leave me here all alone?'

'To be frank, I'd answer "Yes" and "No" in that order to your questions,' I replied, thinking we were coming close to our first disagreement and wondering what else was on Ruth's mind.

'Take Whisper with you, then,' she said, as she rolled away from my embrace and presented me with the first cold shoulder I had known in our relationship.

28

Our reconnaissance party consisted of nine members. There were three swordsmen, Caspar, Raymond and me. Our three bowmen were Bow Master Chun Ging and two monks, Binbin and Ran; our two hand-to-hand warrior monks were Mando and Darma – who also, naturally, acted as interpreter – and our tooth and claw champion was Whisper. With the exception of Whisper, we all carried everything we needed on our backs, in our hands, around our waists or slung across our shoulders.

To hasten our progress over the snow and ice, we attached what could only be called 'snowboards' to our footwear. These were heavily waxed boards of wood about two feet long and a half foot wide, which, once you got your rhythm, stride and weight balanced correctly, enabled you to move swiftly by sliding over the snowscape. They worked nearly as well on the more slippery ice surfaces. Raymond, Caspar and I had quite a few spills before we managed to get our actions and balance right. Both Mando and Binbin had been on the first reconnaissance, and they led the way.

We first sighted the Xi Xia army just over a week later, and as reported, it did not appear in good condition. It was large enough to stretch for slightly less than a half day's march along the valley, but it was in a thin line and not moving very quickly. The vanguard of about two hundred seasoned warriors appeared to be in the best shape, as they were still mounted and sat upright and alert on their ponies' backs. The rest of the horde straggled, struggled and staggered behind them.

'At that rate of march, they'll be about two weeks' trek from the Buddha's Smile,' observed Caspar as we lay just behind the snowline above the valley. To our right towered the third and furthest peak Caspar had marked out in the monastery.

'We need to strike now, before the army passes by,' said Darma, translating for Chun Ging. 'This location is perfect for an ambush avalanche.'

'I had hoped for much more time to prepare such a surprise for our foes,' replied Caspar and then waited again for Darma's back-and-forth translation with Chun Ging.

Caspar's face took on a troubled expression before he offered, 'We could try to start one immediately. My fear is we would all be seen and the enemy would deploy to the other side of the valley before the avalanche was prepared. It would also alert them to our presence.'

Just then, Raymond poked me in the ribs and pointed. 'What on Earth is Whisper doing way up there?'

We all turned our attention from the valley below to see Whisper making her way slowly and cautiously, as if hunting, up the very last few yards of the peak high above us. From the pinnacle there protruded what looked like a table-sized icy shelf. As she approached it, she slowed her pace even further, placing each paw tentatively into the snow and ice before letting it take her weight and bringing another forward to repeat the same wary process. I had no idea what she was up to, nor did anyone else in our party.

Whisper finally reached the crest. Very carefully, she pivoted upon it and presented her tail to the valley. She then issued a lengthy stream of steaming urine onto the junction of the icy overhang and the rock of the peak. As soon as her stream was finished, she bolted down the mountainside as fast as she could.

At first, nothing seemed to happen. Then we heard it – the faint sound of ice cracking and a single loud snap that accompanied the detachment of the overhang from the rock of the peak. The chunk of ice plummeted straight down and hit the snow below it, immediately starting a snowslide that gathered size and momentum until it rapidly became a roaring avalanche.

The Xi Xia army below went into disarray. Some of the warriors tried to escape the avalanche by running or urging their ponies to the front of the march. Others tried to make it to the opposite side of the valley, and some attempted to retreat to the rear. The result was chaos as the ponies and tribesmen became trapped and slowed in the churned-up snow.

It was then that the cascade of rock, ice and snow fell upon them. Almost immediately, half of those directly below us, a good third of their force, disappeared under a cloud of billowing white powder. We could hear the screams of ponies and men as they fought against the smothering icy deluge. This was shortly followed by several adjacent side falls, which saw yet more men and ponies disappear into a cold and pale mass grave.

Eventually, the fall of ice and snow abated, and an eerie silence settled over the scene below us. Our party was still concealed, with just our eyes peeking above the snowline, peering down into the valley.

Of those caught in the avalanche, there were some, but very few, survivors. In places, we could see the snow being disturbed as a hand desperately clawed its way to the surface, to be followed by a head that immediately slumped and began gasping in great lungfuls of air. Up ahead, in the distance, we could see that the vanguard had turned around and was attempting to make some order out of the disaster. Behind the devastation, the rearguard and reserves were doing the same. It was definitely a scene of chaos, confusion and carnage.

'I think,' said Caspar, 'that this little setback will slow the enemy's advance at least for a few days while they search for survivors and salvage what they can from the wreckage. Whisper has done well.'

'Yeah,' said Raymond. 'Piece of piss, wasn't it?'

29

We had just begun to edge our way down the slope, sliding feet-first on our bellies, when Whisper came bounding through the snow, playfully leapt upon my back and pushed my head into the ice-cold powder, as if to say, 'Well, Ippy. What did you think of that little trick?'

I rolled over, grabbed her in a gentle bear hug and let her lick the snow from my face. As we were far enough below the ridgeline, the other members of the group offered her belly rubs, ear scratches and some appreciative pats on the back. Whisper revelled in the attention. All those times she had to turn and pivot to do her business off the terrace balcony during the ice tunnel collapse had reaped an amazing dividend.

Chun Ging offered a comment, which Darma translated as, 'I really could believe this leopard is indeed a messenger of the gods. It is just as well so many of us witnessed what she did up there, because I do not think anyone would believe our story otherwise!'

We all nodded and quietly laughed.

'It's time we made ourselves scarce around here, in case the enemy decide to put out more outriders and scouts,' said Caspar with authority. 'It's a two-day journey back to the next pass, and we'll need to make preparations when we get there. On your feet, gentlemen. Let's get going.'

Raymond and I, as usual, travelled side by side, sharing conversation and humour, of which Raymond was always a rich source.

'How long do you think they'll take to resume their trek?' said Raymond.

'Depends if they saw us or find any signs of our presence, I guess,' came my reply. 'If that's the case, I think that vanguard will be hot on our trail, but I really doubt we were seen or heard. About the best they can do is blame a lone snow leopard who needed to take a piss from a very high place. I suspect at this stage they may see it as an unfortunate accident of nature.'

'Or maybe an act of the gods to warn them away,' added Raymond rather hopefully.

'I wonder which gods they actually do worship, or even if they worship any god at all,' I replied.

Darma overheard the conversation and offered, 'I believe they worship what they call the Sky God and sometimes his partner the Earth Goddess. I do not know by what names they are called.'

We pushed on through the rest of the day, gliding smoothly on our snowboards but leaving a very easily followed trail until a snowfall covered it up. Caspar found a cleft in the mountainside that offered reasonable shelter from the wind and snow. We settled down to a meal of cold rice balls, as Caspar was unwilling to light any fire which might be seen from a long way off and give Xi Xia scouts a clue to our presence and location. After the meal, we settled down as best we could to a rather chilly and uncomfortable night's sleep. *Like so many others we've had in the last week or more,* I thought.

The next morning, we all shook ourselves awake and moved cold and stiff limbs around to get our blood flowing again and help warm us up. It was going to be another bright, clear day, with no sign of snow clouds and, unfortunately, no cover for our tracks.

'Did any of you hear that animal, or whatever it was, making an almighty roaring last night?' asked Raymond of the group as we took a few bites of yet more unheated rice cake for our breakfast. 'I wonder how big the bears grow up here.'

'It was probably Dzu-Teh, the great red bear of the mountains. Some call him Yeh-Teh,' said Darma, who was standing nearby. 'The people of the lower villages have plenty of legends about him, as he is so rarely seen and leaves such large prints in the snow when he passes by. He is the largest of the mountain animals and the deadliest.'

'Well, from the sound of him, I hope he passes us by at a very great distance,' responded Raymond.

'I think Whisper would have alerted us if the beast was dangerously close,' I said.

We packed our gear again and shuffled, slid and glided our way to our next destination, which we reached early that evening. There was still enough light to see that the second pass identified by our reconnaissance scouts was a slightly wider valley with a very long but less steeply inclined slope. Its snow was mostly lightly packed, with little ice or rock mixed in. I thought it would be difficult to start any snowslide or avalanche.

'Not quite the killing ground of Whisper's first ambush,' commented Caspar. 'The trick will be not giving our presence away. We have eliminated much of their central military train, but the rearguard and, more worryingly, the vanguard remain intact. The rearguard seemed the larger force, but the vanguard will contain their most battle-hardened warriors. Any suggestions?'

Chun Ging offered, 'Individually, the monks of our order would match any of the Xi Xia's warriors. Our biggest worry is being swamped and overrun by their superior numbers. If possible, I would vote to eliminate the rearguard and the reserve forces with it. Can we do this?'

'I think we have two or three days to prepare,' answered Caspar. 'Any ideas?' he asked of us again.

I was looking at the slope that led to the peak upon the rise.

It was at least a half mile in length, and I realised a co-ordinated ambush avalanche along its entire span would take out many beneath it, quite probably the entire rearguard and the reserves.

I said so and waited for a response from my comrades. There was silence and consternation at first, and then Binbin began to chuckle to himself and said something that Darma translated as, 'We could snowball them.'

After some initial confusion, Binbin demonstrated how even a small snowball rolling downhill gathers more snow and can quickly become a tumbling boulder capable of launching further adjacent snowslides, and any doubts we may have had were quickly expelled. Fortunately, Binbin's little demonstration looked like a natural snowslide and would not arouse any suspicion from the oncoming Xi Xia. Binbin proposed rolling up a large number of snowballs, placing them at intervals of about a yard along the ridgeline, and, as much as possible, co-ordinating their launch down the slope as the rearguard and reserves rode or strode below us.

It was a good plan but risked our being observed while launching the snowballs. We decided it was worth the risk as we could outrun any pursuit on our swift snowboards. We really had no other choice.

Caspar immediately broke us up into two work parties; three of us would dig and prepare a campsite for the next two or three days, and the rest would commence making snowballs, rolling them up the slope and placing them along the ridgeline every few feet. As the ridgeline was a good half mile long, this proved to be a very time-consuming project, and night quickly fell, so we were unable to work for very long. Learning to roll and pat the snowballs so they did not break and fall apart took some time and effort on my part, particularly with little light.

I have to admit that Raymond was faster and more adept than I at snowballing. As a consequence, he chose to launch a few of his 'balls' in my direction. Even in the face of adversity, Raymond could always find a way to joke and fool around.

30

The second day saw faster progress in setting up our icy artillery, as we had three extra hands, no longer preparing the camp, to assist in the task. Its repetitive nature saw us all become more efficient and proficient at making good-sized snowballs.

By midday, our line of wintry weaponry was nearing completion. Whisper had disappeared for a while in the morning and returned at about this time. There were frozen drops of blood on her whiskers, indicating she had been successful in hunting down some fresh meat. Furthermore, what she had eaten would've been warm. I was jealous. Cold rice cakes didn't really cut it for me, and I was constantly hungry. I knew Raymond and Caspar felt the same from some of our conversation the night before. I suspected the monks wished for some warmth in their bellies as well.

It was as I was considering the steaming, juicy joy of a roasted joint of beef that I heard the first *phhhit* of an arrow speeding by my face. From the corner of my eye, I saw Binbin tumble with an arrow through his neck. It had emerged directly under his chin, having probably severed his spinal cord and sliced through his windpipe. I doubted that he knew what had struck him.

'Attack! We're under attack! Take cover!' I yelled as another *phhhit* passed close by my head. An arrow pierced Chun Ging's neck, causing him to stagger and fall over in the snow. He rolled and kicked, clutching at his neck as blood poured from the wound and from his mouth and nose. It was not the precise shot that had ended Binbin's life so quickly, and it was a little while before he stopped moving.

'Ran, get to cover! They're taking the archers first!' yelled Caspar, not realising Ran didn't understand a word of what he'd said. Darma attempted to repeat the message in the local language, but it was too late. Ran toppled, an arrow in his neck as well. Fortunately for Ran, it was another precise shot, and he died almost immediately.

Caspar and Mando had made it to the ridgeline. They were unable to raise their heads above it, as their silhouetted outlines were an easy target. But they did have good cover. Raymond, Darma and I were caught below and unable to move about, as we did not know where the foe had positioned themselves. I was hiding behind a drift of snow and able to surreptitiously scan the surrounding mountainside. I noticed Whisper lying flat some way away, looking at me as if waiting for something. I gave her the two signs for 'stalk' and 'kill'. Keeping herself low, she turned and slithered off through the snow. She seemed to know where the Xi Xia archer, or archers, lay hidden.

Something had made me wonder whether this was an enemy patrol or an individual scout. I knew each warrior of the steppes could fire off arrows in rapid succession. If there was more than one archer, they would have taken two or more of us out at the same time, rather than just one after the other. I suspected a single archer who obviously favoured the neck shot. But where exactly was he?

I could see Raymond and Darma hiding behind some nearby snowdrifts, keeping their heads down. They were about twenty yards from where I lay.

'Raymond!' I called. 'I think there is only one archer. We need to flush his position. When I give the signal, you and I must quickly jump up and then back down before he can line up a shot and get it off. Darma, keep your eyes scanned for any movement.'

They both nodded, and a moment later, I swept my hand across to the left and jumped up, as did Raymond a split second later.

'I have him,' said Darma. 'He's up behind the drift that has two humps on it, over to the right. About forty yards away.'

We were pinned down and unable to move. There was no point in Raymond and me contemplating any charge on the archer's position, as we would both be dead before we had gone ten paces.

Binbin's body lay very near my position, his bow and quiver still across his shoulders. An idea formed in my head. Binbin's right foot lay a little more than a foot from the edge of my covering drift. By lying flat, I could burrow my arm under the snow to reach his foot and hopefully drag his body, bow and quiver to me. I prayed I had the strength, given the awkward position I would be in.

I was fortunate. The dead monk's body slid easily toward me, despite two arrows quickly hitting the snow around my hand. I removed the bow and quiver from Binbin's lifeless shoulders. The string was wet and useless, but I knew the monks kept spares in the quiver's side pocket. I quickly re-strung the bow and notched an arrow, ready for flight.

I sighted on the drift that Darma had identified and called out to Raymond, 'Do you think you can do another quick jump? I'll try to get in a shot before he can.'

'I bloody hope so!' shouted Raymond in response, laughing. 'On my call this time, okay?'

He gave the signal and leapt up. An arrow nicked his earlobe and pierced the upturned collar of his coat. At the same time as I saw the Xi Xia warrior rise and release his arrow, I released mine. Unfortunately, it was not a kill shot and only succeeded in hitting the warrior's hand, injuring it and sending the bow sliding downhill in the snow.

'Are you alright?' I called to Raymond.

'You might say it was a rather close shave, but I'm okay,' he replied.

'He's lost his bow down the hill. Shall we draw our weapons and take him together?' I asked.

'Sounds good,' said Raymond, slowly standing up and unsheathing his falchion. I did likewise, drawing the long stiletto I had carried since leaving Acre.

Although unarmed, Darma indicated he would charge the Xi Xia warrior along with us as well. I had seen him in hand-to-hand training at the monastery and felt confident the three of us could do the job.

Together, we slowly approached the snowdrift. Raymond and I reached its front, wondering if the archer was still behind it, as there had been no movement. Raymond signed that we should all go over together when suddenly, the drift of snow burst apart before us and a Xi Xia warrior emerged, swinging his sword wildly. The blade swept by only a bare inch from our faces. As Raymond ducked away, he lost his footing and went sliding down the slope, tripping Darma as he did so. I had stumbled backwards away from the blade to slip and fall as well, winding up on my backside in the snow in front of the warrior. He stepped forward and raised his sword above his head for a killing blow. I fruitlessly tried to wriggle out of his reach. Just as I was expecting the blade to slice my skull, two black-and-grey-spotted paws wrapped across the warrior's face and raked their claws over his cheeks and eyes.

This gave me the brief time I needed to jump to my feet and thrust my stiletto to the hilt into his heart. Not just once, but several times. The bastard really had scared the devil out of me, and I was briefly taken over by a rage I never knew I possessed.

Whisper was licking the blood and gel of the warrior's face and eyes from her claws somewhat nonchalantly, as if saving my life was no trouble at all. I knelt down beside her and gave her the most heartfelt hug I could. She wriggled over onto her back, obviously wanting her belly rubbed as well.

I obliged her.

31

Caspar was straight back to business almost immediately, insisting our snowballing work continue as quickly as possible despite the loss of our three archer comrades. There was no need to dig a grave for them. We laid them side by side in the snow, and after Mando and Darma said what I assumed to be brief prayers over them, we left them to be taken by the wild animals and birds of the mountains.

Caspar placed Mando as a lookout, and the four of us – Caspar, Raymond, Darma and I – began the arduous work of completing the long line of snowballs. We laboured solidly through the rest of the day, and by sundown, the work was complete. It was just as well, because Mando came running back to alert us to the fact that the enemy were about two miles further back down the valley. They were making camp for the night.

As we sat around a fireless campsite eating yet more cold rice cakes, Caspar outlined his plan for the next day.

'Tomorrow, we must let the smaller vanguard pass and seek to demolish the much more numerous rearguard, along with their reserves. We shall have to space ourselves equally along the ridge and remain hidden until the rearguard and reserves have entered the killing zone, which stretches from the first snowball half a mile away to just below the peak of the mountain behind us. Then, I will give the signal of a long howl, which should travel the length of the zone. Upon hearing it, you are to run along the ridgeline and dislodge the snowballs as rapidly as you can.

'Sadly, but also fortunately, we will be able to use the snowboards of our fallen friends to aid in shifting the snowballs. You should be able to run by each ball and use the board to flick it over the edge, as opposed to having to stop and push each time. This should speed the process of collapsing the whole line.

'The biggest problem is that we will each be responsible for approximately two hundred yards of ridgeline, and the time it will take us to cover that distance worries me, particularly should any of us lose our footing in our haste. If one of us does slip, do not stop to assist. Keep going. It is the timing of the avalanche that is important. We cannot afford to lose two men when it might have been only one.'

Darma translated this for Mando, who nodded. Secretly, I thought Mando would've liked to have waded into the enemy, taking as many lives as he could and happily giving his own in retribution for the deaths of his three brother monks.

Caspar scratched his chin in thought for a moment then continued, 'If all goes to plan tomorrow and the avalanche is a success, our immediate objective must be to flee as fast as we can back to the relative safety of the Buddha's Smile. The leaders of the vanguard will not be fooled by a second avalanche, and it is very likely that at least one of us will be seen by the enemy. Their army did not stay long at the last ambush site, and I suspect they will immediately seek us out this time around. The pursuit will likely be a cat-and-mouse affair, given we must travel for two days on snowboards and the enemy may have the advantage of their ponies if the snow is not too deep or soft. We can travel faster than those ponies, but not for as long. Any questions?'

'The five of us travelling together on snowboards will leave a trail as clear as day,' I said. 'Mando and Darma know the mountains well. We could split into two groups led by one or the other to get us home by separate routes. This would delay and divide the enemy as they decide which paths to follow and who goes where. Further, Mando and Darma could divide us again by pointing out landmarks to meet up at in the distance. This would again cause the enemy consternation.'

'They might even give up altogether,' offered Raymond rather hopefully.

'I doubt it,' replied Caspar. 'Honour is everything amongst these cultures, and they won't give up the trail so easily – although we can certainly hope so. Ippolito's plan has merit. Let us put it to the vote.'

We had to wait a few minutes while Darma translated to Mando. Mando considered the options then held his hands up, showing two fingers on one hand and three on the other. Darma did likewise. As it was my suggestion, I did the same as well.

'Well, that decides it with no further votes needed,' said Caspar. 'Tomorrow, when we make our dispositions, Raymond, Darma and I will stand closest to the peak and Ippolito, Mando and Whisper will take the rear. This is so we may speedily depart in our separate parties.'

Darma explained this to Mando, who smiled to himself, before offering a comment back. Darma also smiled before informing us, 'Mando is happy. He believes that the messenger of the gods will offer protection to those who travel with her.'

Mando smiled at me and then bowed his head to Whisper. Whisper flicked her tail in response, which sent a spray of snow over our already cold rice cakes.

Caspar was still all business. 'Tomorrow, only take food in your coat pockets, and abandon the packs and anything else that is unnecessary. They will slow you down. Now, I suggest you get what sleep you can. There will not be much had over the next two or three days. The moon is gibbous and will light our way during the night – that is, failing cloud cover. I will take the first watch. Last watch will wake us all an hour before dawn.'

And with that, our business for the next day was complete.

32

'Come on, farty pants. Time to get up.'

This, quickly followed by a gentle booted nudge in the backside, was Raymond's wake-up call to me. The others were stirring around me, and I stretched and wriggled cold, stiff limbs, trying to get some circulation back in my extremities. I completed my ritual and rubbed snow in my face to finish my pre-dawn awakening.

'Caspar says to get a rice cake into you quickly, and then we're setting out straight away to take up positions. Don't forget to grab one of the spare snowboards.'

As the sun came up, we were all in our positions down the extended line of what Raymond had dubbed 'Ambush Ridge'. Caspar was nearest the peak, Darma two hundred yards below him, Raymond likewise below Darma with Mando and me another two hundred yards apart each, bringing up the rear. It was bitterly cold, and I appreciated Whisper's warmth against my body. Of all of us on the ridge, Whisper seemed the most relaxed and had curled up beside me as we waited for the enemy camp to begin its march. They did not take long to stir.

It had snowed a little overnight, and the snowballs looked less evident against the skyline than they had yesterday. I was glad of this, as they had previously appeared somewhat artificial and could have given our ploy away to the enemy. Now they seemed just like natural undulations along a mountain ridge.

Caspar's position, as the highest, offered the best position for viewing the progress of the Xi Xia force as a whole. Mine, at the lowest end of the ridge, allowed me to make out individuals in the ranks, and I marked out who I thought might be men of power and authority.

Only those dozen or so warriors leading the army appeared to have any sort of armour. One in particular wore some kind of protective headgear. It was little more than a metal bowl, but it featured a band of a brighter metal running around its rim. His body armour was the same as those around him. It was a dark brown in colour and was probably treated pony hide moulded to fit its owner's contours. Everyone wore fur-lined leather coats, leggings and boots, whether walking or riding. All carried a bow and quiver full of darkly fletched arrows, while those at the front sported swords and knives in their belts as well. I thought many of them still looked pale and unwell.

Time dragged as I waited for the vanguard to pass beneath my position. They seemed in no hurry, and all were breaking their fast while seated on their ponies, with what looked like strips of meat pulled from under their saddles. Many of them were passing flasks, canteens and skins between them, from which they all drank deeply.

I estimated that the vanguard was at least five hundred strong and wondered whether the monks would really be able to defeat such a number in close-order combat, if it came to that. The odds would be almost five to one. The vanguard travelled mostly in single file, with occasional clutches of two or three riding together in conversation.

Eventually, the vanguard had passed beneath my position, and there followed a gap of about two hundred yards to the leading troops of the rearguard and reserves. I estimated that there were over two thousand warriors spread out just over half a mile. We would have to co-ordinate our ambush to the minute to take out as many of them as possible. It was now up to Caspar to make the call, or rather the howl, to put our plan into action.

The vanguard had moved well past Caspar's position beside the peak and the rearguard were moving up beneath him. Even in the ice and snow, I could feel my palms sweating as I waited to hear the wolf's howl. I looked up the line of the ridge and could see the others peering up to Caspar as well, waiting, no doubt, in a similar anxious state to mine.

Then it came – a long, clear and carrying wolf's howl.

Immediately, the five of us were all up, snowboards in hand, dislodging snowball after snowball as we hurried by them, running as fast as we could along the slippery slope. Sprinting uphill through snow on an inclined surface, even with snowboards, is very tiring and a huge strain on the leg muscles. Mine were burning as I passed my halfway mark. While I did not look back at my own balls tumbling down the ridge, I could see, ahead of me and below into the valley, that our strategy was working.

All was chaos in the column as ponies reeled and reared in panic. Warriors ran into each other and fought to get by each other. At regular distances, waves or large boulders of snow crashed into the column, and pocket after pocket of troops disappeared under the wash of white.

I kept running, dislodging the remaining snowballs in my stretch of the line, and finally reached the end of it. I could see Mando had finished his run, and ahead, the others were coming to the end of theirs. This time, I did stop to catch my breath and surveyed the whole scene below. The vast majority of the rearguard and the reserves had disappeared under a mountainside of snow. Only a few stragglers at the very end of the line had survived and been saved from a suffocating, chilly death.

Up ahead in the distance, the vanguard had stopped and were looking back at the destruction. Then, as Caspar had predicted, they turned and spurred their ponies up the slope in our direction. We had obviously been seen, or someone in charge had a suspicion there were saboteurs on the mountain.

It was time for us to flee for our lives.

33

Mando slid on his snowboards quickly down the slope to my position. I turned and waved a good luck salute to Raymond, who had been joined by Darma and Caspar. Then we turned and took off in different directions with all haste.

Mando led the way with Whisper and me following behind. Our path at first was clear: down the other side of the ridge to the valley below and then back in the direction the army had come from. This was a tactical decision to throw the Xi Xia off our track. Hopefully, they would not be expecting us to do this.

We made very good speed upon the firmly packed snow, and looking back, I could see no sign of pursuit – yet. There was still the problem that we were leaving a trail for a pursuit party to follow. Snowfall would be the only chance of obscuring it. Unfortunately for us, the skies above were clear. Not a cloud in sight.

Initially, Whisper bounded through the snow, keeping equal pace with Mando and me on our snowboards. After an hour or more, I noticed she was tiring and beginning to fall behind. I called out to Mando, and we halted briefly while I picked Whisper up and laid her across my shoulders, noticing as I did that she was getting heavier, just as Ruth had said. She quickly settled there and did not move once she had a stable position. Mando smiled his understanding. Then we were off again.

For hour after hour, we pushed ourselves, with only a few limited breaks after crossing over some very steep and exhausting ridges. It was after the last and longest ridge that we looked down over a very broad valley that stretched away into the distance. Mando indicated we would now be travelling this route. I looked back along the route we had followed. I was surprised there was still no sign of pursuit.

I set Whisper down on the snow, and she immediately began scampering and bounding around us, eager to be off again. Mando indicated that we could slow the pace, as we would need to conserve our energy for the rest of the day and probably the night ahead. We naturally travelled mostly in silence, as neither of us knew any words in the other's tongue. We did well enough with a basic sign language that developed as we went along.

We did not stop for any meal breaks. Instead, we just reached into our pockets and took bites of rice cake to keep us going. Whisper disappeared for a short while in the early evening, returning with a number of small and bloodied white feathers still clinging to her coat in places.

Mando indicated we should take a slightly extended break. Both of us were able to convey with signs and facial expressions that our legs were taut and burning with pain and fatigue. The place he chose for our rest was a good one, with clear views both ways up and down the wide valley. Again, there was no sign of pursuit. I said a small prayer of thanks in my heart for this further reprieve.

Eventually, all good things must come to an end, and we got up, ready to begin again. The sun was setting at the western end of the valley in a blaze of reds, oranges and yellows that reflected off the snow and mountainsides, while a gibbous moon filled the eastern night sky with a softer silver light. The valley took on a magical aspect in those brief moments as the light changed in colour and intensity.

We embarked on the night leg of our long retreat. The gibbous moon set halfway through the night, and we continued on by starlight, still in a westerly direction along the valley floor. I was carrying a sleeping Whisper on my shoulders again but did not mind the extra weight, as I had got my second wind and felt I could walk all night. Mando seemed to have rallied his spirit as well, as we glided and slid over the smooth snow at a good pace.

I could feel one of the straps around my snowboard coming lose and hailed Mando for a stop. He turned around and pulled up next to me, and we both went to rest on a more solid-looking snowdrift where I could adjust and re-tie the straps of my board. Just as we sat down on the drift, we were thrown back off it as it rose and roared to reveal an enraged Dzu-Teh, the great red bear of the Himalayas.

Mando and I rolled to opposite sides of the great beast, who had reared up on his hind legs and stood over seven feet tall. Whisper was now wide awake and hissing loudly back at him. He gave another loud roar as he shook the snow from his shaggy coat and cast his eyes about for who or whatever had disturbed his rest. His eyes fell on Mando, who was immediately up and away on his snowboards.

Despite his huge size, the bear was remarkably fast as he lumbered after Mando. Whisper followed him, swiping and biting at his back legs but only occasionally distracting him from his quarry. His winter pelt was simply too thick for Whisper's claws and teeth to penetrate.

I quickly got my snowboard re-attached and took off in pursuit as well. I had no idea what I was going to do or how Mando and I could escape the beast. Whisper obviously had some ideas, for in the next moment, she had leapt upon the bear's back and was attacking his head and neck with claws and teeth. Using the back of his paw, Dzu-Teh swept Whisper from his shoulders, sending her flying in a tumbling ball of fur and snow. I was relieved that upon landing, she immediately righted herself and recommenced her attack, this time on his back legs again. Despite her valiant attempts, Dzu-Teh was gaining on Mando, who cast a quick and frightened look back over his shoulder to see the bear only a few yards behind him.

He should not have looked back. He did not see the shallow dip in the valley floor that caused him to stumble and slow his pace. Whisper leapt again onto the beast's back, getting her claws into his face and eyes just as his great paw raked its way down the length of Mando's back, easily ripping through clothes and flesh to expose vertebrae, ribs and shredded muscles in a great spray of blood.

The beast roared in blind rage as Whisper leapt from his back before another paw could dislodge her. The great bear stumbled around blindly, bellowing in pain, his wild thrashing preventing me from reaching Mando's side. Whisper kept up her harassment on the bear's left side, forcing him to the right and away from us, allowing me to reach Mando.

He was in a very bad way and bleeding profusely. There was nothing we could say to each other. He looked at me with pleading eyes, indicated the stiletto by my side and pointed to himself.

I knew I had to. I knew he wanted me to. I did it quickly.

Whisper continued her harassment of the bear, scoring many bites and slashes to his blinded body. He too was losing a lot of blood from his emptied eye sockets and the myriad of wounds Whisper had left upon him. I raced in behind the monster and, slashing my stiletto behind both his knee joints, hamstrung him in another gush of blood.

With an almighty roar, Dzu-Teh buckled at the knees, crumpled and fell backwards onto the snow. I watched as Whisper sprang and sank her fangs into his neck to tear away at the great artery running through it. It was only a few minutes until the great beast lay still.

Whisper trotted over to me, and we both sat down in the snow, her head in my lap. She was breathing heavily from her exertions. I quickly ran my eyes and hands over her body, seeking any injuries.

There were none; it seemed she did have the luck of the gods. All I could think of was poor Mando, and then I had an even more disturbing thought. I was somewhere in the middle of a somewhere I did not know!

There were two things I had to do before I left Mando and Dzu-Teh and continued west. First, I went over to Mando, removed the remaining rice cakes from his coat pocket and placed them in my own. Second, I drew my stiletto and approached Dzu-Teh. For some reason, I felt obliged to beg the beast's pardon for what I was about to do. I used the stiletto to sever one of his great fore-claws. It was too big to fit in my pocket, so I placed the bloody appendage down the front of my coat and tightened my belt so it did not fall out.

I decided there was no time to offer Mando to the sky as, even though there was no sign of pursuit, I did not know how far away the enemy might be. I was also worried all the reeking bear and human blood around me would draw other dangerous carnivores to our location.

By the time I had finished my work, Whisper had recovered her breath and energy and appeared eager to be gone as well. Instead of trusting to my own instincts and sense of direction, I called her to my side. I said one word, 'Ruth', and made the sign for her. Whisper looked at me as if to say, 'Well, of course, dimwit!'

With that, she turned around and led me home.

34

Whisper did not disappoint me. She guided me through the rest of the night and into the next morning, always heading west, until we arrived at a mountainous cul-de-sac at the end of the valley. Whisper chose the northern face, and we started our ascent. I was desperately tired by this time but kept myself going. I was relieved when, halfway up the slope, I looked back down the valley and realised I could see for miles and miles and there was still no sign of any pursuit. I was now convinced the vanguard must have gone solely after Caspar's party. I prayed that they would be resting at the Buddha's Smile by now, safe and unharmed.

I decided that I could afford to have a rest myself and indicated this to Whisper by lying down against a convenient rock. I must have dropped off to sleep for a while, as when I awoke, Whisper was demolishing the last of a small snow hare. I said a little prayer of thanks to Mando and tried to enjoy a cold rice cake I had taken from his pocket before Whisper and I set out again.

It was mid-afternoon when we arrived at the ice cave entrance to the monastery. Our approach had been observed, and Ruth, along with Masters Po, Do and Dari, was waiting at the entrance to welcome us home. Ruth and I immediately fell into a marvellous embrace, which was made even better by Whisper wriggling herself between us, simply wanting to share the love to which she was most readily welcome.

Ruth and I finally disengaged, and Master Dari was the first to ask, 'Where are the others? What has happened?'

I was about to offer a reply but was interrupted by Li Po, who said, 'Let us get them both inside and warmed up first. The boy is almost blue with cold!'

I noticed the wonderful warmth of the rock tunnel almost straight away and was happy to make our way to the dining hall.

As we arrived, Kali guided a still shaky and unsteady Hadar into the hall. Once we were all seated, and I was holding a mug of hot, savoury vegetable broth, I related the events of the last several days. The amazing story of Whisper's piss and the resultant avalanche which fell upon the Xi Xia army brought some gasps of amazement and a few laughs; however, the ambush and deaths of Master Chun Ging, Ran and Binbin ended the mirth. The encounter Raymond and I had with the lone archer scout and how Whisper saved me from the scout's deathblow held my audience in tense silence. The making of the snowball artillery wall, with its accompanying results, received a small cheer. Finally, I told the story of our decision to split up, Mando and Dzu-Teh's deaths and Whisper's leading me home. It certainly was a long and eventful account.

I had just placed Dzu-Teh's claw upon the table when the sound of the alarm gong echoed down the corridors and into the hall. Warrior monks armed with staves and bows seemed to appear from everywhere, making their rapid way back to the ice cave entrance. Master Dari must have organised all of them to be on stand-by alert. We hurried to follow.

As we gained the outside of the ice cave, the cause of the alarm became apparent. The other members of our party were arriving back at the monastery but were still a hundred or so yards away and very closely followed by the entire vanguard of pony-riding Xi Xia warriors. The archer monks immediately set themselves into rows and sent a hail of arrows raining past the heads of our three friends and into the warriors' front ranks. A dozen or more riders and ponies went down, obstructing those behind them. It was enough to give our three comrades time to draw away from their pursuit.

As they approached, it became apparent that Raymond and Darma were supporting a slumped Caspar between them. The archer monks continued to fire with deadly accuracy, leaving dozens more Xi Xia dead and forcing the vanguard to retreat. This allowed Raymond, Darma and Caspar to make it to the comparative safety of the ice cave. It was only then that we could see a black fletched arrow protruding from Caspar's lower spine.

'To the infirmary, quickly,' said Ruth, as the archer monks continued their now-sporadic shooting to keep the Xi Xia at bay.

Caspar and Darma did not relinquish their support of Caspar and continued their awkward gait through the corridors that led to the infirmary. Once there, they gently laid him on his front on the examination bench, the arrow's feathers pointing to the ceiling.

'Caspar? Can you hear me?' asked Ruth.

'Yes,' came a weak reply.

'Can you move your legs?

'No.'

'Can you feel this?' said Ruth, as she pinched the skin of his calf through his leggings.

'Feel what?'

Ruth took a scalpel and sliced open the back of Caspar's coat and vest to reveal the arrow embedded in his spine. It had passed between two of the lower vertebrae. It did not seem to be buried deeply, but it had been very destructive.

'Ooth an Do. Take row now out,' said Hadar, forgetting to sign.

Ruth and Master Do washed their hands and forearms in spirits of wine. They also washed a heavy pair of tongs before applying Do's unguent around the wound site. Master Do took the tongs, gripped the arrow at its nearest point to the skin and lifted it up and out in one easy motion. Ruth immediately applied pressure to the wound, and the slight blood flow soon ceased, enabling her to place a clean dressing over the puncture site.

I helped Raymond, Kali and Darma transfer Caspar from the examination bench to a cot in the infirmary proper. As we laid him on his side, he passed urine in the bed. He seemed unaware that this had happened until he noticed the spreading dark stain at his front. He was acutely embarrassed and ashamed of having done so, especially as Raymond and I had to change both him and the bed linen.

'I'm so sorry. So sorry,' he kept saying, almost unable to look at us.

'Forget about it,' said Raymond. 'I always said you were a pisspot.'

Master Do went to a cupboard and removed a small cushion about a foot long and six inches around. He explained it was filled with a fluid-absorbing moss and would help keep Caspar dry should any further accidents occur. He placed it over Caspar's crotch and gently pressed it down into place, moulding it over the area.

Caspar appeared despondent and asked pointedly, 'I'll never walk again, will I?'

It was Master Do who simply replied, 'No.'

'And the bladder? The bowels? Like just before?'

Master Do just nodded his head to this, as if it would minimise the stark reality of Caspar's current and future state.

I could tell Caspar was thinking it would also, on his return to Jerusalem, mean there would be no future with Isabella.

35

We left Caspar in the care of Master Do and the two monks in the infirmary. It was clear Caspar wanted to be alone with his thoughts for a while. A warrior reduced to an invalid was a cruel fate. I prayed Caspar would rise above it and find some further purpose and contentment in his life. In the meantime, we had to deal with the fact that our principal military commander was out of action.

Raymond and I had only a few moments to greet each other with great brotherly slaps on the back and a rib-crushing hug. Ruth interrupted our reunion and said, with some authority, 'We had best check the situation at the ice cave entrance. Grab your weapons.'

She turned and briskly led the way like a true warrior queen.

The monks and the Xi Xia had reached a stand-off at the entrance. The Xi Xia had moved back out of our bowshot but were still within the range of their own much more powerful bows. Eight archer monks held the line just inside the entrance. They were reinforced by a dozen or more behind them, ready to step in should one fall. Even so, it appeared that the greater numbers of Xi Xia and the further range of their arrows would lead to the attrition of our own archers.

I saw an opportunity to enhance our defence and suggested that those in the front line fire from bended knee, while those behind fire from an upright position, thus doubling their power. The monks saw the advantage and immediately took up the deployment. Master Dari looked a little embarrassed that he had not seen this obvious improvement. Just then, four monks arrived carrying wooden tabletops to act as mantelets and provide a protective shield across the entrance, thereby strengthening our defences even more.

'Master Dari has had everyone busy preparing defences and laying traps in case the monastery is actually penetrated by the Xi Xia,' Ruth informed Raymond and me. 'There are mantelets stored at each fallback position within the complex, along with two or three of these.' She indicated two pottery jars with what looked like wicks protruding from their necks. 'They are filled with spirits of wine. You light the wick and throw the jar at the enemy. When it breaks, the spirits of wine ignite and explode. If you find yourself using one, try to make it smash high on a wall or against the ceiling so the flaming spirits fall on those below – hopefully, only the Xi Xia.'

I picked up one of the jars and turned it over in my hand. It was a good weight for throwing a fair distance.

'Note the extra staves, quivers and bows stored here as well,' said Ruth, pointing out the small armoury. 'Lastly, Raymond, you'll be pleased to note this bag. It contains caltrops. Unfortunately, the monastery doesn't have a smith or foundry; the caltrops are poorly made, and there are only limited numbers available at each defensive position. They should penetrate a sheepskin boot but would be crushed under a pony's hoof. It was I who explained and suggested them to Master Dari after telling him of your exploits at Gadaraghatta.'

'I'm impressed by all this preparation,' I said. 'It seems you and Master Dari have indeed kept everyone busy. Let us hope it is enough.'

'Well, I don't know about you two,' said Raymond, 'but what I need right now is some sleep. I'll see you at the evening council meeting. That is, unless the alarm gong sounds first.' With that, he made his way to the dormitory.

I looked at Ruth, who was playfully scratching Whisper's ear.

'I thought a lot about you during the quiet moments and on our long marches,' I said, as we continued along the corridor.

'And I about you,' she replied. 'I'm glad that Whisper was with you. It seems my trust in her was not misplaced.'

'Indeed,' I said. 'I owe her my life and our mission's success. I swear I could almost believe what Li Po said about her being a messenger of the gods and the familiar of shamans and physicians.'

We walked on in comfortable silence and arrived at the balcony terrace, stepping out into its cool, airy embrace. Far below, we could see the baggage train and wagons of the Xi Xia. I doubted that any of the people below knew that two thirds of their warriors had been wiped out by just eight men and a wily snow leopard. Still, our wins over the last week or so had taken their toll on us. There was the loss of Ran and his master Chun Ging. I thought of smiling Binbin and how he never got to see his plan for the snowball artillery come to fruition. Mando's death still lay heavily on my mind, even though I knew I had done what he wanted and what was humane, given his horrendous wounds and the circumstances we were in. And then there was Caspar, lying in despair in the infirmary.

I suddenly felt my eyes welling with tears, and a lump formed in my throat that would not let me speak.

Ruth looked at me. Her eyes said everything that needed to be said between us right then. She took my hand without a word, and we made our way to where we could have some privacy.

Intimacy can be a wonderful healer. It was too bad I fell straight to sleep.

36

Things at the ice cave entrance remained at an impasse for the next few days. Every now and then, an occasional frustrated bowshot would punctuate the deadlock. The Xi Xia could not advance into the ice cave any more than eight abreast, which was not enough to break through the line of sixteen bowmen and the stout wooden mantelets defending their position. The numerous scattered bodies of dead Xi Xia lying in and around the entrance were witness to the ineffectiveness of their offensive assaults, as well as testament to the monks' defensive organisation and skill. The main problem facing us was that just as the Xi Xia could not enter our realm, neither could we escape it.

As it turned out, the Xi Xia had been busy cutting the tails and manes from their ponies and making two very long ropes. They secured the horsehair ropes to rocks on the summit, high above the red balcony of the Buddha's Smile. From there, they were able to lower themselves down to the balcony terrace. They did this in the middle of the night, and only a sleepless monk who had decided that some fresh air might help him sleep was able to alert the monastery. He saw the silhouettes of the first Xi Xia dropping onto the balcony, ran yelling and screaming, and roused the monastery by beating the alarm gong as rapidly and as loudly as he could.

Within minutes, all was chaos within the monastery. Armed and unarmed monks hurried to assembly points as Master Dari directed others to determine where the action was. Some time passed before the sleepless monk was able to locate Master Dari and tell him where the enemy incursion was actually taking place.

It was to our advantage that the Xi Xia were intent on consolidating their numbers within the balcony hall before spreading out through the monastery. While this allowed the Xi Xia to gather a large force inside, it also gave Master Dari time to organise his defence.

Ruth, Raymond, Kali and I attached ourselves to a band of stave fighters taking a stand in the corridor outside the infirmary. It was not far from the balcony terrace where the Xi Xia were grouping. Fortunately, only a few of them could descend the ropes at one time, but even so, there were at least twenty gathered with weapons drawn in the balcony hall by the time we began assembling.

The staves the monks held were different to the smooth poles we had used in practice. Each had a short, hooked blade at both ends. Raymond had the forethought to trade his falchion for Caspar's broadsword while we were outside the infirmary. All of us would have to be conscious of our comrades' positions in the upcoming fracas, with so many deadly bladed weapons whirling around in the confined space. I grabbed a spare stave from the pile by the fallback position. Ruth was armed with eight throwing knives, and I gave her my stiletto. I felt she was very under-armed compared to the rest of us, but the presence of Whisper by her side gave me some confidence. Even so, I insisted that she take a position to our rear and pick her targets carefully.

Suddenly, with a loud yell, the assembled Xi Xia charged into the corridor. Our band charged back at them with staves held to the front and lunged as a mass into them, sending many sprawling back across the floor and into their comrades. I came with our second wave, slicing the blade of my stave across the throats and into the bodies of as many of the downed warriors as I could. Ruth stood at the rear, skilfully picking her targets. I watched as Kali saved Raymond's neck by ramming his stave into the face of a warrior who was beating Raymond down with heavy sword blows. The speed of our attack had neutralised their use of the bow, and they were reduced to the less familiar swords and knives they wore at their waists. Raymond, Kali and the monks at the front had their long staves and a broadsword, giving them the clear advantage of reach.

Gradually, we forced the Xi Xia back the way they had come, and then they broke and ran. We did not follow. Master Dari had made it clear to our squad the defence of the infirmary was our primary role. We picked up and assisted three of our wounded back to the infirmary, where Hadar, Li Po and a couple of other monks were already treating the wounds of two monks injured early in the fight. Caspar had insisted on being sat up in a chair and placed by the door. He held Raymond's falchion, ready to defend those with him in the infirmary and fight to the death if needed. I hoped it was not an actual death wish. We placed our wounded on the cots and left as quickly as we had arrived to take up our positions again.

We were facing the way the enemy had come before, and it was not until we heard Ruth's shout of alarm from our rear that we became aware they were rapidly approaching from behind our position. Ruth quickly expended her last three knives in securing her escape back through our ranks, where Whisper assumed a protective stance in front of her once again. The attack from the rear could only mean one thing – the archers' defence of the ice cave entrance had failed. This was devastatingly bad news for us. We were now caught between two groups of enemy Xi Xia.

Again, we charged with staves held forward and hit the enemy before they could fire a second volley. Their first, however, took a heavy toll on our front line, with most falling, dead or wounded, leaving only ten of us standing to fight off this new assault. We were clearly outnumbered, but again, we had the advantage of the extra reach of sword and stave. I entered the fray, using the sharpened billhook of my stave to slice the necks of any Xi Xia I could reach, or painfully wrench and drag them to the ground, where sharp claws and teeth quickly finished them off. I realised that Ruth must have directed Whisper to look out for me and not her.

Raymond and I stood side by side for quite a while and managed to bring down many of the Xi Xia, but more and more of them kept coming. Our squad was rapidly becoming depleted, and things looked grim for us. Were these my last moments on Earth? I looked around for Ruth and did not see her but had to turn back quickly to the fight. Two more monks fell beside Raymond and me, when I heard Ruth's voice scream, 'Get down!'

She was running down the corridor with one of the jars of spirits of wine, its wick spluttering dangerously close to its brim. Raymond dragged the remaining monk still standing down with him. I leapt onto Whisper and held her still, just as Ruth hurled the jar against the wall adjacent to the leading Xi Xia warriors. The jar shattered in an explosion of flame that enveloped the warriors, turning them into human torches that staggered blindly about, shrieking in pain. Many turned and careened into their comrades, either setting them on fire as well or causing them to retreat.

The stench of burning flesh and clothes in the confined corridor was nauseating and reached painfully into our lungs. Despite the suffocating and blinding smoke, I lunged and lunged the billhook of my stave into so many burning and disoriented Xi Xia that I lost count of those I had slain. I could hear Raymond's grunts of exertion as he swung Caspar's great broadsword like a windmill, slicing heads, arms and legs from their bodies. There was a pile of corpses and limbs growing around us.

Suddenly, there were no more warriors alive in front of us. Only Raymond and I were left still standing in the corridor outside the infirmary. Beside the dead and dying bodies of the Xi Xia lay the corpses of the remaining monks in our group, who had made their last stand fighting beside us.

Raymond and I looked at each other in the sudden silence and momentarily laughed at each other. We were both splattered in blood and gore from head to foot. I felt as though I would never be able to catch my breath, despite panting so heavily and rapidly.

Our respite was a short one, as shouts and fierce yells from further down the tunnel indicated that a fresh and unburned Xi Xia force was heading in our direction. I scanned around for Ruth and Whisper, but they were not in sight, nor was there an answer when I called out Ruth's name. I hoped they were safe and unscathed somewhere.

'The infirmary,' coughed Raymond, as he made for the door. We burst in, surrounded by a cloud of smoke, slammed the door shut and proceeded to barricade it with the remaining cots. It would hold against warriors trying to shoulder their way in but perhaps not the fire if it spread. Only then did I have time to notice that the infirmary had been filling up with wounded monks, many of them groaning in pain from hideous wounds. I made a rough guess, given the failure of the ice cave entrance, that we were likely down to half our compliment of warrior monks.

Hadar, Master Do, Chandra and another monk were busy tending to the wounded. They, like Raymond and me, were covered in splattered blood. I was relieved when Ruth and Whisper entered the infirmary though a side storeroom door.

Hadar looked up from his needlework and managed to say, 'Hall. Fight. Baaad.'

'Did Master Dari leave any stores here?' asked Ruth, to which Hadar pointed his needle at the corner. There lay a small sack of caltrops and three of the incendiary jars. Raymond grabbed the sack, Ruth and I took an incendiary jar each, and the monk who had been helping Hadar picked up the third. As one, we turned and quickly left through the supply door.

We could hear the sounds and screams of intense fighting before we turned the first corner that led to the hall. The fighting there must have been a convoluted back-and-forth affair, as when we entered, it was not to join our comrades but to find ourselves directly behind the battling Xi Xia.

Even though the hall was too packed to risk the incendiaries without harming our own people, this was a stroke of extremely good fortune in a night that had been devoid of luck for most of the monks. Raymond moved quickly, throwing a spray of caltrops under those at the rear of the melee. I tried not to laugh at the almost immediate result of the Xi Xia warriors hopping about in pain on their punctured feet. This made them easy and vulnerable targets for my billhook. Raymond gave the bag to Ruth for further judicious casts of the caltrops and joined me as we waded into the Xi Xia with broadsword and stave, and together, we began our slaughter once again.

Whisper was kept busy with fang and claw upon those who fell to the floor. I saw one Xi Xia with his hands around her neck, trying to throttle her, while she held his throat in her jaws. One quick twist and shake of her head and the Xi Xia's hands fell away from her and he lay dead. Raymond and I were covered in even more splattered blood as we slashed our relentless way into the foe. In a matter of minutes, the remaining monks had rallied, and we forced the Xi Xia from the dining hall and back down the corridor.

I felt the battle's fortunes turning back in our favour as more and more Xi Xia found themselves cornered in the balcony hall, caught in a four-way trap between us, the enraged monks, their few still-burning comrades and the great drop from the terrace balcony. Master Dari was there, directing the monks to contain the Xi Xia in the hall but not enter it, simply preventing them from leaving and attacking again. Ruth stood by him, holding an incendiary jar. Master Dari lit it with a torch and Ruth tossed it up into the air to land in an explosive fire around and behind those nearest the exit.

Blinded and disoriented by the flames consuming them, those who tried to escape the hall were goaded back with billhooks.

Two more incendiary jars set all the Xi Xia in the balcony hall on fire. It then became a simple matter of prodding the hapless, burning Xi Xia warriors onto the balcony and over the side, where they fell in flaming trails to crash in a spray of sparks onto the wagons of their baggage train far below, igniting many of them in what became an exceptional fiery climax to the whole encounter.

37

There was not much time to enjoy the pyrotechnics below, as a number of small fires burned within the monastery that needed extinguishing. Master Dari was again all business, ordering squads to flush out those Xi Xia who may have escaped the conflagration and been hiding within, awaiting an opportunity for revenge or to escape the monastery and flee to the hills.

The first place Ruth, Raymond and I went to inspect was the infirmary, where we found Hadar and Master Do attending to the wounded in their calm, quiet and efficient manner. Hadar was no longer standing but seated as he saw to the repair of the monks' broken bodies. Caspar had put aside his falchion but was keen to hear the details of the fight.

'I could hear so much of it but couldn't see it, and, of course, I could do nothing much anyway,' he finished with an obvious ruefulness.

Raymond obliged him with a brief account of our part in the conflict but was unable to give the details of the battle in other parts of the monastery, as we had not seen or heard any reports of the events in other places. He promised Caspar he would come back and tell him the details once we had completed the sweep of the monastery. We said our farewells and continued on.

The fight at the entrance to the ice cave must have been intense. All the archer monks that had been positioned there were dead, but a far, far greater number of Xi Xia lay around and in front of them. All the monks were pincushioned with arrows; many had been hit three or four times before they had finally fallen.

It was much the same in the main hall, where we had seen battle ourselves and turned the tide with the roughly made caltrops. Across the floor, the dead Xi Xia outnumbered the monks, some of the bodies showing hideous wounds. The smell of blood and emptied bowels was overpowering. There was very little ventilation in the hall to clear the odours, unlike on a fresh-air battlefield. The stench would linger there for quite a while.

Similar scenes emerged along the corridors and tunnels where skirmishes had been fought. The number of Xi Xia dead outnumbered the monks in all locations. The monks' bodies showed signs of having fought on despite sustaining serious wounds.

Squads of monks were detailed to remove the dead Xi Xia. They were unceremoniously dragged to the terrace balcony and thrown over to land on the still-smouldering baggage train below. They would not be honoured with any Sky Burial.

It was later during the clean-up that Hadar approached Raymond and me and signed, 'You two. Take one dead Xi Xia body. Put body outside monastery. Place in the snow. Bury. We find later. Show. Teach you more on body.'

Hadar then turned and hurried away, back to the infirmary.

Raymond and I did as requested, dragging one of the Xi Xia bodies from the ice cave entrance, covering it over with snow and placing a broken stave as a marker in the mound.

'Why would Hadar want us to keep one of the Xi Xia buried outside like this?' queried Raymond.

'I'm pretty sure that Ruth and I might be in for another anatomy lesson or two,' I replied.

The bodies of the dead monks were set aside in a dignified

manner for a funeral service and Sky Burial once the mopping up was complete. All were placed in the Hall of the Golden Buddhas until then. Miraculously, the hall, and – more importantly for the monks – the Buddhas had remained untouched by the flames and hostilities.

There was one upside to the battle, aside from our victory, which was that the monastery came into possession of several dozen tailless and maneless ponies. Many others had simply scattered during the battle. There was also some speculation about what may be left behind in the wreckage of the baggage train once the surviving Xi Xia in the valley moved on. They would not be able to take everything they had plundered from their previous raids, due to the damage and destruction of so many of their wagons.

The Xi Xia would remember the warrior monks of the Buddha's Smile for a long time.

Several Xi Xia were found hiding in the halls and tunnels. Some chose to fight and were swiftly despatched. Li Po had declared that any Xi Xia who surrendered peacefully were to be spared and released. Only two chose to surrender – they were the only survivors from a force of close to five hundred. Before releasing them, Master Dari insisted on slicing off the second and third fingers of their right hands so they would never be able to draw an arrow again.

Late in the evening, at the end of what had been an exhausting day, we heard the gong sound once again and made our way to the prayer hall. Li Po and Master Dari were about to address the very much reduced number of monks and our own small party. Darma found us at the back of the hall. His arm was in a sling and one eye was closed due to a massive bruise on the side of his face. Despite this, he was in good spirits and kept up a whispered translation for us.

Li Po opened the meeting with a prayer, one of thanks to the Buddha for the deliverance of the monastery and the surviving monks. This was followed by another prayer for the peaceful repose of the monks' dead brothers, the seriously wounded in the infirmary and those who were troubled by what they had seen and been forced to do that day. He then thanked all present for their courage, perseverance and warrior spirit.

Li Po was followed by Master Dari, who delivered similar words of praise. He then presented the 'butcher's bill' to us. He did not begin with the number of monks who had died that day. He began by naming each of the deceased, mentioning their discipline of expertise and how long they had served the monastery. It was a long list, and I recognised the names of monks I had come to know and like in the time I had been there. From the expressions on Ruth and Raymond's faces, I could tell they too were reflecting on the loss of people who had become their friends.

Master Dari eventually reached the end of the long roll call of deceased and then listed the seriously wounded in the infirmary, exhorting the monks to pray for their recovery. He ended rather bluntly, simply stating, 'Sixty-seven of our brother monks died today. This includes the entire division of our archer monks. Master Do tells me two of our brothers will not survive the night. Our surviving complement of unharmed or only slightly wounded is sixty-three. We have lost over half our number.' And with that, he sat down, looking old and very careworn.

Li Po stood up and bade everyone to get a good night's sleep, as there was much to be done in the way of cleaning up and farewelling the monks who had died that day.

We did not go back to our beds, but rather to the infirmary, where Hadar was helping Li Po close up the last of the wounds that needed suturing. They both looked very tired, and I noticed that Hadar had a pronounced tremor in his left hand. A sure sign that he was fatigued. Ruth and I helped the pair to tie the final sutures, and then we all made our separate ways to our beds.

38

As predicted by Master Dari the evening before, the two seriously
wounded monks died overnight, bringing the death toll from the
Xi Xia attack to sixty-nine. Along with their dead brother monks,
the two bodies were reverently placed in the Hall of the Golden
Buddhas to await what I thought would be some kind of mass Sky
Burial or, as the situation possibly demanded, mass cremation.

When Ruth and I finally pulled our aching and weary bodies
out of bed somewhat later in the morning than usual, the first
thing we noticed was that there did not appear to be any monks
moving around the monastery. We did not see or hear a single one.

'This is strange,' observed Ruth.

'I know,' I replied. 'Let's check the infirmary first.'

When we entered the infirmary, Hadar and Caspar were sitting
in quiet conversation while Raymond and Kali helped one of the
wounded monks to stand.

'Where is everyone?' I asked, after greeting them.

'The monks are all in the Hall of the Golden Buddhas,' answered
Caspar. 'They're having some kind of mass funeral service for the
dead. We felt it discreet not to intrude on their rituals, and there
still are the wounded in here who need attention and care. However,
Darma did say it wouldn't be an issue for us to attend, as the monks

say we have earned their respect and have shown the same to them. Nothing like a victory in battle to bond warriors together.'

'I should like to show my respect to the dead monks,' said Ruth. 'I had grown to like a number of them, and after all, as you say, we were all comrades in arms.'

'I too,' I added.

'And that includes me as well,' said Raymond.

'Very well. You did fight beside them,' said Caspar. 'Hadar, Kali and I will look after the remaining monks in the infirmary. There are some things I can still do to help out around here and not be completely useless.'

He said the last with only a trace of pique.

Raymond, Ruth and I left and made our way to the Hall of the Golden Buddhas. Halfway there, Whisper silently joined our group. The doors of the great hall were open when we arrived, so the four of us were able to discretely enter and take a seat on the floor at the rear of the hall, from where we could watch the proceedings.

The deceased monks had all been washed, dressed in new robes and placed in rows behind Li Po. The service and rituals were similar to those of Shen Wee's funeral service: Li Po leading the monks in prayer, the twirling of the prayer cylinders and the vocal orchestrations from the throats of the monks.

This vocal orchestration went on for a while, but when it ended, it stopped suddenly, to be replaced by the total silence of all present. At a given signal from Li Po, groups comprised of six monks arose. As one, they approached their allocated deceased brother, bowed respectfully to him and hoisted the body onto their shoulders in one fluid movement. I realised that this was made easier by the fact that the bodies would be in a state of rigor mortis. This rigidity made them easier to lift and manage than a normally flaccid unconscious body would be.

Given the proportions of monks dead, alive and wounded or incapacitated, only eight of the laid-out deceased were lifted at a time. Once all eight were suitably elevated onto their bearers' shoulders, Li Po led the cortege from the hall. Raymond, Ruth, Whisper and I moved aside respectfully as the party passed through the door, and then we silently trailed behind.

The cortege moved through the halls and corridors till it exited from the ice cave entrance. From there, the line of bearers made its way up the nearest peak. As had happened at Shen Wee's funeral, every so often, one of the monks would blow a long, mournful note on an ornate and somewhat oversized brass horn as if announcing to the sky and heavens that the dead were on their way.

It was after about an hour of slow and respectful climbing that we neared the summit. Once there, Li Po motioned for a halt and the deceased were gently laid upon the snow. More prayers were said, punctuated with twirling and tinkling prayer cylinders and deep-throated vocalisations, before the party turned around and headed back down the slope to the monastery.

Eight more corteges would make their way from the Hall of the Golden Buddhas to the high summit of the nearby peak, and it would take all day. For some unspoken reason between the four of us, we walked behind each of the processions to pay our respects to our fallen comrades. By the time we brought the last bodies to the summit, we could see that the true Sky Burial had begun. High overhead, a number of vultures and some other unidentifiable birds were slowly circling above the burial ground. Down below, on our earthly plane, some of the deceased bodies were missing eyes and displayed shredded cheeks and lips. No doubt other, larger mountain scavengers would continue with their part in the Sky Burial during the night.

Needless to say, we were all hungry and tired after climbing to the summit many times that day. I thought of how much more exhausted the bearers would have been. The four of us went straight back to the infirmary to check on Hadar, Caspar and Kali. They had not experienced any problems while we had been away.

Naturally, they were curious about the mass Sky Burial, and we related all that we had seen of the farewell to so many monks.

Ruth commented, with some distress, that it had personally upset her to see that so many of her deceased 'comrades in arms' were to be eaten by wild animals and birds. She said Shen Wee's Sky Burial had not had this effect upon her.

'Do you think it was our last trip to the mountain and seeing the final aspects of the monks' Sky Burial?' I asked of her.

'Probably,' she answered.

'When in Rome,' commented the ever-pragmatic Caspar.

Raymond, always wanting the last jest, offered, 'I think there will be some fat and well-fed scavengers hanging around the mountains for quite a while, with all that food lying up there.'

39

Despite their defeat, the Xi Xia left some legacies behind to further blight the monks and us. The first was the extensive damage to the internal environment of the monks' living arrangements. The removal of much of the timber from around the monastery to shore up and secure the ice tunnel had depleted much of the wood. Most of what had been left was damaged by the fires created by the incendiary pots that had been used so effectively against the enemy. Unfortunately, floors, wall panels, shelving, furniture, drapes, bedding and much more were irreversibly damaged by fire or smoke. Despite so many flaming bodies being forced to exit over the terrace balcony, the timber of its structure, being very hard and solid, was only slightly charred, and the balcony was still structurally sound.

The monks, along with Kali, Raymond, Ruth and me, set about the dirty business of stripping and removing the burned timber. At the end of each day, the four of us were grey-faced from all the ash floating around in the atmosphere. The airborne ash also made us cough, irritated our nasal passages and produced red, itchy eyes, not to mention all the minor cuts and abrasions that came with the rough manual work.

The dirty work was complete within a week – stripped, swept

and washed clean. With the exception of the kitchen, infirmary and Hall of the Golden Buddhas, the floors, walls and ceilings of nearly every hall, dormitory, study and corridor were now bare rock. Ruth and I noticed that the monastery seemed to become colder, particularly at night.

Early on in the clean-up, Li Po had delegated a small group of monks to visit and negotiate with the villagers of the lower valleys for the supply of new timber to refurbish the interior of the monastery. The villagers were aware that the monks' victory at the Buddha's Smile had saved their own lives and their homes from sacking and pillaging by the Xi Xia. They were both grateful to the monks and equally saddened by their losses. Consequently, the villagers were happy to contribute the necessary timber for the repairs to the monastery, and it was less than two weeks before teams of them were hauling timber up the mountain. Amongst them were artisans carrying sacks of tools and nails to assist in the reconstruction.

Darma pointed out that such generosity and co-operation from the villagers was not only an act of appreciation and thanks but also part of earning advancement along the path to enlightenment and, eventually, nirvana. It worked both ways.

The second legacy that the Xi Xia left behind for the monks was more serious than a simple clean up and repair job. The first signs of it began to appear in the second week after the defeat of the Xi Xia. Initially, the disease manifested as rash-like symptoms, beginning as small pimple-like nodules that a few days later turned into larger, blackened spots of dead skin.

Master Do recognised the disease by the dark spots that were appearing on just about everyone. 'This can be very serious,' he told Hadar, Ruth and me in the infirmary. 'I was wrong when I suggested the Xi Xia were suffering from altitude sickness. These black spots are bites from an insect and cause an illness that is called either Chagas disease or Dai-Phus. Some of us will get quite sick, while others will suffer less serious symptoms. From my experience, I expect the next stages of the disease to appear in the next few days.'

'Wo… wo…. wot?' stuttered Hadar, not using his hands.

'Everyone will suffer headaches. That is the first and most universal symptom. Most will progress to disturbances of the gut, with nausea, vomiting and the watery flux. Fever often accompanies this stage as well. For those who are severely affected, they can become confused and unsteady on their feet, as if affected by alcohol. It was these symptoms we observed in the Xi Xia. Even more alarming is that some will probably succumb to complications of the heart and lungs. A few may cease passing urine or enter into a coma from which they may or may not awake.'

'How do we treat this disease?' I asked worriedly, as I scratched at one of the itching bites on my arm. 'I remember seeing lots of little red-brown insects moving around in the dirt and dust during the clean-up. They were everywhere.'

'We cannot cure it; we can only let it run its course and treat the symptoms as effectively as we can. The best we can try to do is eradicate the insects in our environment so they do not keep re-infecting everyone.'

'How do we do that?' I asked, still scratching.

'An even more thorough cleansing of the monastery with the hottest water we can manage, infused with the oils of some herbs I have in my store. Smoking them out using the same herbal oils on the fuel will eliminate them as well.'

'Master Do,' enquired Ruth, 'would it be a good idea for all the monks to take extended baths in the grottoes below us and wash all their clothes and bedding? The water is very hot and full of salts and minerals that might be detrimental to these insects.'

'An excellent idea, and a good place to start, Ruth,' came Master Do's appraisal of Ruth's suggestion. 'As you are the only female here, I suggest that you take the first bath and wash your clothes as soon as you can. I will direct the monks to do the same later in the day.'

With that, Ruth and Whisper departed the infirmary. I wondered if Ruth was going to try and entice Whisper to have a bath as well. She did not mind the snow but never showed any liking for water.

'Master Hadar and Sir Caspar,' said Master Do, 'the Xi Xia were not able to enter the infirmary, and you have hardly left the room. You are both more vulnerable to the possible ravages of Chagas. After you bathe this evening, I would like you to quarantine yourselves in here until the contagion has passed. While you are bathing, I will have the rooms treated to remove any insects.'

This was not greeted with a great deal of enthusiasm by either Hadar or Caspar, but both accepted the necessity, as neither wished to contract any serious form of the disease.

That evening in the grottoes was a great success in washing ourselves, our clothing and our bedding free of the bugs; it also killed them. Whether it was the hot water or the salts and minerals or both, I do not know, but after an hour, the surface of the water was dotted with the dead bodies of the nasty little creatures. Li Po decreed that until the monastery had been totally cleansed, we and all monks were to wash ourselves at the end of each working day. These evening bathing sessions soon became occasions of great mirth amongst the monks, who laughed and played and dunked each other. After everything those in the monastery had been through, it was therapeutic to let off a bit of steam, have some fun and wash away the horrors of the Xi Xia invasion.

40

I was not surprised when, two mornings later, I woke up with a splitting headache, feeling so nauseous I vomited shortly after. Ruth checked me over and said I was running a fever. As well as this, three of the bites I'd received had necrosed and turned into black spots about the size of my little fingernail. Apart from in the aftermath of Gadaraghatta, I had never felt so terrible.

Shortly after Ruth had insisted I stay in bed and drink plenty of water, a sweating and very pale Raymond staggered into our room, a black spot clearly visible on his neck.

'I'm sick, and I can't go to the infirmary, as Hadar and Caspar are quarantined in there and I might still have bugs,' he said, and then looked at me, adding, 'Oh, hell. You're sick too.'

'I am unaffected at the moment,' said Ruth. 'I'll have to look after the pair of you. Raymond, the bed is big enough. Get in it with Ippy, please.'

'If you fart under here, I swear I'll spew all over you,' I said, commencing what was to be several days of lively badinage between us, despite the fact we both felt as sick as dogs.

Ruth came and went, followed by Whisper, who remained close to her at all times. Strangely, Whisper had taken to rubbing herself up against Ruth in some way at every opportunity she had. Ruth reported the cleansing of the monastery was well under way, using both Master Do's herbal oils and hot water from the grottoes, and smoking had been undertaken in all the communal areas as well. She said a number of monks were unwell, some noticeably sicker than others. All were being treated and isolated in their dormitories and sleeping areas. Unfortunately, Master Do had also succumbed to the disease, and only Ruth, Kali and Chandra were available to treat the sick, which necessitated Darma having to work with them to translate. Ruth estimated that at least twenty of the monks were bedridden, with six others only mildly affected by headaches or slight nausea. Ruth said she would have been run off her feet if it had not been for the healthy unaffected monks also taking it upon themselves to assist their brothers despite the supposed quarantine. Hadar, Caspar and Kali remained free of symptoms.

One fortunate aspect of the situation was that the nausea most were experiencing greatly dampened any desire for food, while the fever merely created a greater thirst for water. This obviously made catering to the nutritional needs of the sick a lot easier for those working in the kitchen. Ruth told Raymond and me that most of her work involved providing cool sponges and ice packs to bring down the raging fevers that some were experiencing. Aside from this, Ruth was happy to report that none of the monks had developed any of the life-threatening symptoms that Master Do had outlined. I put this down to the healthy lifestyle that they lived and said so to Ruth, while Whisper was again rubbing herself against Ruth's arms.

'It's strange,' said Ruth, 'the way Whisper keeps doing this. At first, I thought she might have been traumatised by the battle with the Xi Xia and seeking some comfort and reassurance, but she is such a heroic and fearless warrior that I somehow doubt this. I've started thinking she might be doing something else.'

'Like what?' asked Raymond.

'Well, her fur would be a natural attraction for those insects causing the Chagas disease. Yet I have inspected her all over – in every nook and cranny of her paws and claws, inside her mouth, nostrils and ears, even under her tail – and there are no insects or signs of their dirt on her at all.'

'You must have washed her well in the grottoes,' I said.

Ruth burst out laughing at this. 'You should have seen her wriggling and fighting me the moment I picked her up and went to place her in the water. I'm surprised you didn't hear the caterwauling. She was definitely not going in the water or near it, so I didn't get to wash her. It has made me wonder if she has some sort of inborn insect deterrent in her fur or secreted from her skin, like sweat.'

'I suppose it is possible,' I said.

'I know it sounds strange, but given everything else this amazing animal has done, do you think this recent rubbing against me has been her way of deterring the insects? I think she knows exactly what she's doing. She is protecting me.'

Whisper continued her movement against Ruth as if to emphasise her evaluation.

'The evidence of my eyes tells me you are right,' I said. 'I believe it.'

'So do I,' agreed Raymond.

41

Two weeks saw the Chagas disease run its course through the monastery, with only a handful of monks further succumbing to it and no one dying of any unwanted complications, for which we were all grateful. There had been enough death in the Buddha's Smile. Caspar and Hadar were more than happy to be released from their protective quarantine, as were I and the secretively farting Raymond. I was very glad to have him out of my bed and Ruth back in it. She and Whisper had been sleeping on a mat on the floor by my side for over two weeks.

Upon being notified that it was safe to do so, the village artisans returned with their tools and, alongside the monks, finally set about finishing the refurbishment of the monastery. The women of the villages had been busy during this time as well, and Li Po was presented with newly sewn robes, bedding, cushions, and floor coverings, along with two beautiful wall hangings representing the Lord Buddha in many of his different manifestations. These were hung in a place of honour in the Hall of the Golden Buddhas, much to the beaming pride of the women, who gathered when the wall hangings were ceremonially put in place.

Li Po was clearly very pleased that the Buddha's Smile had survived the biggest known threat to its existence in its history. What was more, the monastery had been reborn, which was symbolic within the monks' spirituality and way of looking at the world. Many of them said they felt a greater holiness and peace about the place and felt closer to a state of enlightenment as a consequence.

It also had an effect on Caspar. The artisans of the village had seen his immobility and had made him a special chair with four wheels where its legs should have been. His two strong arms, which had wielded a great heavy broadsword in battle, had no problems wheeling him independently around the monastery. He was limited to its interior but did not seem to mind this minor shortfall. It seemed that every time I encountered him, he was engaged with one of the monks in deep conversations, which I did not interrupt or inquire about but suspect were of a personal and spiritual nature. Hadar had informed Ruth and me that Caspar was still trying to come to terms with his disability and was 'wrestling with some of his inner demons'. Caspar had told Hadar he found much of what the monks believed was helping him resolve his issues and anger.

Hadar seemed to have found something within himself as well and appeared to have accepted the limitations of his speech and the weaknesses of his right-side limbs. He still had to rely on sign language to augment his actual speech, but he would often laugh at the tangled words and sentences that came out of his mouth from time to time. With some help from Ruth and me, Chandra, Darma, Masters Po and Do and others in the community had even made inroads into learning some of the sign language.

The only disappointment I observed in Hadar was on the day he summoned Ruth and me for another class in the dissection and discussion of human anatomy. Master Do joined us at his request as well. Unfortunately for Hadar, wild animals had discovered the body of the hidden Xi Xia he had planned to use for our tuition. The birds and beasts had completed their version of the Xi Xia warrior's Sky Burial. I think Hadar took it as a sign that there was no more he could teach Ruth and me.

I held some concern for Kali. Back in Hind, he had taken us all under his wing, had initially procured what we needed for our survival and wants, taught us the different customs, languages and dialects of Hind, advised us how to proceed in new and difficult situations, learned skills of nursing and caring to assist our work and been a cheerful and courageous companion when required. He seemed to have a permanent wistfulness and a faraway look about him, as if his mind was elsewhere and he was wanting to be there.

Life for Raymond and me was much the same as it was prior to the Xi Xia visitation. We continued our daily routine of martial arts training, becoming more proficient in the skills of archery, using the staves and, most recently, unarmed combat, using just our hands and feet as weapons. Raymond was beside himself with satisfaction the day he fractured a board with a powerful mind-driven chop of his hand, as was I a week later.

It was Ruth who first sensed that change was coming upon us, but she said she did not have the words to explain how, why or when. She said she just had 'a feeling'.

<h1 style="text-align:center">42</h1>

Not long after, Ruth's 'feeling' crept its way into my mind as well. For some reason, it happened as I walked into the library, where Hadar, Caspar, Li Po and Master Do had their heads together in a quiet but serious conversation. They became aware of my presence at the same time, and their conversation suddenly ceased in an awkward silence, as if to say 'Oops, we don't want him to hear this.'

Master Do was quick to make it all sound innocent, saying, 'Well, that should solve the issue between them.'

I politely greeted them but felt awkward about my intrusion and moved to the rear of the library, out of earshot, and pretended to be interested in some scrolls that I could not even read. It was a rather pathetic attempt at trying to appear unconcerned and nonchalant. I loitered at the back of the library until, shortly afterwards, I heard the party break up and depart. Within myself, I felt a little bit hurt that there could be secrets between Hadar and the masters that were being kept from me and Ruth, despite everything we had all been through together.

'They may have been discussing something confidential about the other monks,' commented Ruth, after I had told her about my experience in the library.

'But why should Hadar, or Caspar, have that kind of input in

Masters Do and Po's decision-making?' I answered, still feeling let down.

'I have to admit that I don't know. I do not believe that they would wish us ill. It's probably something to do with our education in healing. Or,' she cheekily quipped, 'given that we sleep as man and wife, they might be wanting us to get married!'

With that, she smiled at her jest and poked me in the ribs. I felt my concerns abating. I had no objections to being married to Ruth. In my mind, we were already soul partners for life.

Even so, the feeling that something was afoot stayed with me. I even asked Raymond if he felt Hadar and Caspar might be keeping something from us and explained my reasons why.

Raymond answered, 'I have not felt or seen anything to make me think so. All I can say is that since the Xi Xia assault, they have spent a lot of time together. I had assumed that they were offering mutual support to each other in dealing with, or just talking about, their separate afflictions. Both their lives have been turned around by injury, after all.'

Despite the plausibility of what Raymond had said, my uneasiness stayed with me. I hated feeling this way when it involved two people I had come to both love and respect.

It was two days later, as I was attending some restocking duties in the apothecary and infirmary, when Hadar walked in.

'Greetings, young Ipp,' he signed, without trying to speak the phrase.

'Good morning, Hadar,' I replied. 'How are you today?'

'Fine, fine,' he both signed and said this time, then continued, 'I have been thinking about the future. I think we should all meet up first thing tomorrow morning here in the infirmary to discuss some ideas and plans. Will you ask Ruth and Raymond to come along as well?'

'Not a problem,' I replied, thinking that my feelings and suspicions may have been correct after all.

***

As agreed, we all met early the next morning in the infirmary. Hadar, Caspar and Kali were already present and seated. Ruth, Raymond and I took the remaining three cushions that had been placed in a circle on the floor.

As team leader, and being able to speak clearly for all, Caspar opened the proceedings.

'Things change in life,' he said slowly, as if contemplating each word, 'and change is creeping up on us again. The time is coming for the separation of our ways, and' – he turned to us three younger ones – 'it is for the best of all.'

'What!' exclaimed Ruth. 'What do you mean?'

'Firstly,' responded Caspar, 'Kali wishes to leave us and return home to his village.'

'With the exception of our short visit,' Kali tentatively began, 'I have not been home in over three decades. Now, knowing I have only one sister surviving from my family, I feel a strong wish to return to her and the people of my village. I have felt this way for a while now, although it hurts me to break the bonds of friendship I have with all of you, knowing I will probably never see you again.'

I think everyone present understood Kali's position and feelings on the matter and, in their hearts, could only wish him well.

'I will miss you, Kali,' I said. 'You have been a helpful and cheerful companion. Someday I look forward to showing my children and grandchildren the card tricks you have taught me and telling them all about you.'

Kali bowed his head, brought his palms together monk-style and said, 'I thank you, Ippolito, and all of you for your understanding in this matter, even though there is a terrible pain in my heart.'

'So, it is now just the five of us,' stated Raymond, 'and our mission has been aborted, as there is no cure for leprosy here or in

India. Does this mean we can return at last to Jerusalem? We have been gone the best part of four years.'

Hadar and Caspar cast a knowing glance at each other that spoke of something different.

It was Caspar who spoke first. 'I will not be returning to Jerusalem, or anywhere else, with you.'

'But, Caspar, you are one of us. I won't leave you,' exclaimed Raymond. It was very apparent that he still maintained a squire's loyalty to the knight he had served, fought alongside and helped save from the Xi Xia.

'Nor I,' said Ruth. 'You have led us since the death of Godfrey. We owe you so much.'

'I stand with Raymond and Ruth,' I added.

'Believe me,' said Caspar, obviously holding back some emotion, 'I will not return to Jerusalem or to the Hospital of St Jean. I am crippled. I piss and shit myself and am too great a burden to leave this place. I do not wish to return to the knights in Jerusalem and be the subject of their pity and charity. Nor could I bring myself to beg from strangers and others in the streets. It is a fate I could not bear. In truth, I would prefer death to such ignominy.

'But those are my personal reasons for not going back to Jerusalem. Speaking as your commander, I would ask you, how do you intend to get me safely back home in my condition? I would not only be a hinderance to your progress, I would also be placing your lives in danger. From a military and tactical standpoint, I would order you to leave a liability such as myself behind, albeit with a knife in my hand. I will not ask for the knife, as I now see there may be some real purpose to my staying put that I perhaps do not fully understand yet. Li Po has been guiding me in this. So, there you are. I am sorry to be losing such comrades and friends as yourselves, but it must be as I am ordering you to do.'

Ruth had tears in her eyes, Raymond's were glistening with moisture and I was only just holding my own tears back. Ruth threw her arms around Caspar and hugged him to her, saying, 'I will always remember and love you for everything. The knives you taught me to throw have saved my life and others' on plenty of occasions. I can't thank you enough just for that alone.'

She turned away, releasing him as she did. Raymond had become silent, and I knew he would say a personal farewell to Caspar later on, as I would.

The three of us sat without speaking, not sure what to say or do next.

It was Hadar who broke the silence. His face was clearly showing his own emotions were overcoming him, as his signing and speech lost their synchronicity.

'Body of mine. Too old. Too broken. Too slow. Too much in pain. Down fall me is down fall you too. Like Caspar, it no good for me to leave monastery. This home be for me now. Stay. Talk Caspar. Talk Po. Talk Do. I be happy for that.'

This was too much for me, and my tears really did start to flow, as did Ruth's all over again.

I started to say, 'So we are staying…' but Hadar put his hand up, holding me to silence.

'Ippy, Wooth. Must go. Ray too. Keep safe you.'

'No, no. I won't,' protested Ruth, between sobs. 'My heart is breaking.'

Mine was too.

'Look me,' commanded Hadar. 'Ippy! Wooth! Great power for heal. Bring good. Bring help. Sick get better. Poor help have. World be better by Ippy and Wooth.'

Hadar's face took on a sterner aspect, his voice increasing in volume. 'Why me teach? Why show you? Time is waste me if you not help heal. Same Po say. Po say Dubbha give you to world. You go to world. You must GO!'

Tears were streaming quietly down my face, as they were on Ruth's.

'Hadar, Li Po, Master Do and I have spoken about all of this,' said Caspar. 'Not only do you have a great store of western medicine and healing, but Master Do says you have learned more than he thought possible in such a short period of time. He says the aspects of eastern healing that you have learned here will enhance and compliment those of the west. The pair of you are meant to be healers of the world, not hermits upon a mountain.

'Think of all the good you could do. Think of the people you could save. The women you could bring to a safe delivery. The children who will live to an older age. The elderly relieved of their pains. To stay here for the love of Hadar and me is to deny the world a greater love and a greater gift. You must go.'

'But the way home is blocked to us,' I protested. 'Naiki Devi may still be suffering her demons, and Mohammed of Ghor will not have forgotten us.'

I was desperately clawing for excuses and reasons to stay.

'Li Po says there is another way for you to get home. He calls it the Watery Way, and it is mostly by boat along rivers and across seas. The route will bring you to the Red Sea and then overland back to Jerusalem. He will explain all of this to you tomorrow.'

By this stage, Caspar was the only dry-eyed person in the room. Hadar was wiping his eyes with the cuff of his sleeve, and Raymond was glassy eyed with unshed tears welling between his eyelids.

It was not the final goodbye, but it was certainly the overture.

43

Whisper was waiting to greet Ruth and me in our room. Ruth had let her out to hunt earlier in the day while we met with the others. She must have known, or sensed, that both Ruth and I were upset, and she seemed to make a point of giving us both affectionate licks about the face and hands. Raymond joined us a few minutes later. He received a lick as well.

'Just how are the three of us – sorry, Whisper – the four of us going to find our way back to Jerusalem from here?' asked Raymond. 'I mean, do you know where we even are exactly? Why must they send us away?' He was clearly still hurt and bewildered by all that had transpired earlier.

'I understand their reasons,' I said, 'and I know Ruth does too. Their reasoning is all about the two of us wanting to become physicians. If we stay in the Buddha's Smile, both Hadar and Master Kan Do will have wasted all their considerable time and effort in teaching us to be healers. The vision Ruth and I share of a free hospital for the poor would be nothing more than a pipe dream.'

'I know you're right,' admitted Raymond. 'It just pains me so much right now.'

I could see his eyes turning glassy again. Whisper went over to him and licked his hands again.

'I knew when Caspar took the arrow in his spine and became crippled that he would not wish to return to the Hospitallers or Jerusalem.' Raymond paused, a perplexed look upon his face. 'In truth, I'm surprised that he said he wishes to exercise patience and learn the reason for his injuries. I don't understand that part.'

'I think he has been listening to the teachings of the monks,' offered Ruth. 'He has certainly spent some time talking with Li Po. The monks' religion seems to give them a greater acceptance of what life dishes out to them, as opposed to others in this world, who seem to want everything and anything they can get their hands on. It has something to do with eliminating desire.'

'I think you've been having some chats with them as well,' I commented.

'That is true. It is an interesting religion or philosophy of life, but we must be patient, because we cannot change anything right now and wasting time on worry is pointless. Let us wait and see what Li Po has to say to us tomorrow.'

The next morning, we did not meet in the infirmary. Instead, first thing, we met in Li Po's room, with its view of the west from the balcony terrace. Caspar had been carried in, as one of the axles on the wheeled chair the villagers had made for him needed some minor adjustments. Darma and one of the monks were fixing the problem for him. Hadar and Kali followed us into the room a few minutes later. Whisper went and seated herself at Li Po's feet, where she received her expected scratch behind the ears.

Li Po opened the proceedings. 'I have spoken at length with Hadar and Caspar and understand the reasons for their decision to stay within the Buddha's Smile and send you young people back out into the world. Painful as I know it is for the three of you, your combined destinies are to return to your world. There, you will see the realisation of your dreams of becoming healers. It is also for the fruition of Hadar and Kan Do's visions for you both. This is your fate and the path you must follow. You cannot deny it. Have you accepted this?'

Somehow, overnight, all three of us had separately resolved within ourselves that this sad thing must be, and we reluctantly bowed our heads in the affirmative. Hadar gave us a pleased nod.

'It is as expected, then,' said Li Po. He paused, and then continued, 'Your journey here was long and arduous as well as dangerous. You have faced many obstacles and have overcome physical, mental, emotional and spiritual challenges. I believe it is possible for your journey home to be much less difficult.'

Again, he paused to consider his words.

'I have spoken with Kali, and he has agreed to guide you to his village and beyond to the river not many days north of there. While it is not a great river here, high in the foothills of the mountains, it does run all the way to the sea. It is known by various names along its path, but the most common are the Indus or the Sindhu River. Once you reach the sea, there is a trading port not far up the coast. You should easily be able to gain passage on a ship bound for the Red Sea.'

'But how are three of us to make all this happen?' I interjected. 'How are we to buy, build or borrow a boat to navigate our way down the river?'

'Firstly, Darma wishes to take the wandering mendicant path for a while and has my blessing for this undertaking. It is he who will guide you along the Indus River valley and accompany you to the coast. He will be able to assist with translation, as he knows this part of Hind well. It is where he originally comes from.' Li Po paused here and acknowledged Darma with a smile. 'He hopes to bring the message of the Buddha to those who have not heard it.'

Darma smiled at us and bowed his head. Raymond looked particularly pleased that he was to join us. I suspect the two had developed a bond of friendship and respect as a consequence of the time they had worked together so gallantly to bring Caspar safely back to the monastery.

'Secondly,' continued Li Po, 'Master Hadar informs me he still has most of the money the Emir of the city you stayed in gave you. He wants you to have it for the needs of your journey, which includes the purchase of a small boat.'

'We not spend much in Hind and not spend here,' injected Hadar, not using his hands. 'Plenty money still. I not need it here.' I wondered if he was getting forgetful or lazy about using his hands to augment his communication.

Li Po continued, 'When Kali returns to his village, Darma will take you down the Indus Water Road to the sea and then on to the trading port. The money will not only purchase you a river boat but will also buy you passage on a trading vessel to one of the Red Sea ports. Hopefully, from there, you can join a caravan and return to your home.'

I felt a bit annoyed that this had all been previously worked out amongst them without any input from Ruth, Raymond or me.

'So, when do you propose we commence this expedition?' I asked.

'The spring melt is just beginning. Your departure needs to be timed so that the higher waters of the first melt take you above the rocks and hazards that abound in the winter months, when the river is lower, before the greater spring melt turns it into a wild torrent that is also hazardous and difficult to navigate. Once you have descended from the foothills of the mountains to the plains below, this will not be a problem, as the Indus becomes a wide, placid and slowly flowing river. As to your question, you must be ready to leave at the week's end, in five days' time.'

Reluctantly, Ruth, Raymond and I acquiesced to this.

At this point, Whisper left Li Po and wandered over to Hadar, where she assumed the same position she had at Li Po's feet. I felt she was trying to say something with this action.

Li Po hesitated and then reluctantly said, 'There is one other matter, and it pains me to bring it up. Whisper will not be able to join you on the journey.'

'No,' said an immediately upset Ruth.

I, too, wanted to protest.

'Ruth, you must understand that Whisper is a creature of the mountains and the cold. You will be going back to the heat, humidity and disease of the southern lands. No snow leopard can live in such places. You can be sure she will sicken and die before your journey's end.

'I believe the gods have already spoken to her and she understands. As you can see' – he pointed to Whisper dozing at Hadar's feet – 'she will adopt the role of spirit guardian and familiar to Hadar's shaman spirit. She will look after him for you in your absence.'

'Oh, Whisper,' sobbed Ruth, 'I understand. It just hurts.'

I knew just how she felt.

'There one thing other,' said Hadar. 'Wooth. Be wisest wise woman.'

Here, Hadar began to sign, making sure he was understood.

'Seek to find Trota of Salerno. Important. For women's health reasons. Wooth must study with her. Ippy should study too. Only then can you make the hospital for all the poor – men and women.'

Trota of Salerno – *Who? Where?* I thought.

My head was a jumble of the grief and shock of departure and farewell, as well as anxiety about the dangers of another epic trek. At least there were two certainties: Raymond's enduring friendship and Ruth's undying love. These would see us through.

Acknowledgements

It is an hour's round trip to the nearest town with a bookshop from the little village I live in. Consequently, many sales of my first book, *On Scimitars and Scalpels*, relied on the encouragement and generosity of the following local businesses that kindly displayed and sold my novel.

First, I must thank the mammoth effort of the friendly staff at Malua Bay Foodworks. Matt, Craig, Karen, Katey, Peta, James and Davo – I cannot thank you enough for your efforts. I also wish to thank Dan Wilson of The Moorings Resort at Tomakin and Jason Delaney of Pacific Furniture and Bedding in Batemans Bay.

I also owe a debt of gratitude to the team at Shawline Publishing for their guidance, support, great artwork and professional advice for a new author bumbling his way through the brain fog of long Covid. Aidan, you have the patience of a saint!

Further thanks must go to Grame Fletcher, Bill Legge and Vicki Smith for their ongoing friendship, support and encouragement.

Shawline Publishing Group Pty Ltd
www.shawlinepublishing.com.au

SHAWLINE
PUBLISHING
GROUP